THE OLD MAN IN THE HOLE

"You all know about my gold! Well, I'm gonna give that gold to you!"

The old man standing on the bar was pallid, blue-lipped, with yellowing eyes and a corona of white hair and beard all the way around his craggy face. But the Thompson submachine gun in his gnarled hands was well oiled and ready. He tossed ten gold plates into the crowd. "The maps are on these. Whoever gits there first gits the gold!"

Traveler looked down at the gold plate in his hand. A lot of men would die for that gold. The smart thing to do would be to pitch it into the gutter. *Yeah. But a Traveler could do a lot of traveling with all that bullion.*

That's when he saw the three Road Wasps coming toward him. . . .

ROAD WAR

D. B. DRUMM

A DELL BOOK

Published by
Dell Publishing Co., Inc.
1 Dag Hammarskjold Plaza
New York, New York 10017

Dell ® TM 681510, Dell Publishing Co., Inc.

ISBN: 0-440-17471-6

Printed in the United States of America

First printing—February 1985

D D

PROLOGUE

The Road Predators

He was riding the aftershocks. Civilization had collapsed and its collapse sent out shock waves and the man they called Traveler rode the shock waves like a highway surfer.

He was an automotive savage. Using the dying machinery of a dead society to fight tooth and nail for survival.

He was a highway nomad. He was a post holocaust hunter-and-gatherer.

He was a man trying to forget he had a past.

Normally, he was a loner. But back there, in a miniature holocaust, a blood-soaked killing ground that had been his vengeful confrontation with Colonel Vallone and what remained of the United States Army, he'd found an ally. A partner. The man was called simply Link. He was a big, bald, hard-eyed, wisecracking black man of undeterminable age, wearing tatters but carrying himself like an Ethiopian emperor.

They rode the much-patched-up black van south, along the highway, sometimes along mere traces of what had been a highway, slowly bulling through drifts of sand, circling around craters in the road, cautiously avoiding wrecks—which were often trap-lures—and sometimes having to get out and fill three-foot-deep potholes with rock where the road and desert around them was impassable.

Doing this, they'd take shifts; one man would stand watchful guard with an assault rifle while the other worked. Because the road was perverse. The road was like a coral reef, a place where predators swam up and down, feeding on whatever the road had to offer.

Roadrats. Mutants. Road cannibals. Highwaymen. A nightmarish variety of predators, haunting the blasted wastelands of America, scouring its cracked, half-buried roads for victims. Preying on one another, and anything else that swam their way.

And yet it had been three days, and Link and Traveler had seen almost no one. They'd seen a harmless caravan of nomadic scavengers moving with painful slowness down the road in their horse-drawn, engineless station wagons. They'd zipped past them, Traveler scrupulously avoiding unnecessary contact with other people. Contact with people always led to an adventure.

He'd had a bellyful of adventures.

But he was about to have another.

1

Is It Called an Ambush
If You Know It's Coming?

There had been no trouble in three days. Someone with less experience on the road might have relaxed, let down their guard, deciding it would be an easy trip. Traveler knew better. The road was a living thing to Traveler. It was a sadistic demigod just waiting for him to lower his guard so it could have its fun with him. . . .

Traveler was driving the compact black van; Link was riding shotgun. It was nearly sunset. They were barreling south through a strip of particularly barren desert. The only relief from the monotonous yellow-gray of the Nevada desert was the occasional ravine or dry wash. Or the wrecked, stripped cars by the roadside, every few miles, some of them showing the yellowed bones of ambush victims in their charred cabs.

Traveler gunned past with hardly a side-glance.

Oh, he had seen bodies. He had seen corpses piled thirty feet high. The blast victims, the burn victims, the radiation victims, the victims of famine and the plague that had come after the Third World War. He had not seen the bodies of his wife and children, however. He'd been away, in a countryside military hospital when the ICBMs hit the New York area. And there hadn't been anything left of his family to bury. His home had been too close to the center of the blast. His wife, his child, the house, the whole neighborhood, the whole suburb— all had been reduced to black dust and glass in a charred crater.

But he hardly ever thought about that anymore. It had been fifteen years. And over those years he'd learned to avoid thinking about what he'd lost. If you kept moving, kept traveling, kept distracting yourself with new places, you didn't have to think about the past. You were too busy.

Like, for instance . . .

The telltale glimmer of steel in that ravine up ahead.

Traveler slammed on the brakes.

Link looked at him, startled.

Thirty yards ahead the road became an overpass over the ravine. The steel-reinforced overpass was still intact, at least so far as they could see. . . .

"Ambush," Traveler said. "You see metal, down in that ravine?"

"No."

"That's how I know it's an ambush and not just a wreck down there. The metal moved."

" 'Cause I don't see it now and you saw it before? Okay. But maybe it's some harmless scavengers. . . ."

Traveler looked at him.

"I guess you're right," Link said, as Traveler reached to the gun rack on the interior wall behind him and grabbed his AR15. He'd lucked onto a crate of 5.56-mm ammo for this beautiful little assault rifle, so it was the weapon of choice.

Link had one of the M16s they'd captured from the Glory Boys.

In a way, the black van—the Meat Wagon, Traveler called it—was like a Brink's armored car. It was well stocked with ammo, which Traveler had taken with him as pay after his last merc job, and ammo was a rarity, a trading currency, good as gold. And the Meat Wagon was armored, with hanging bullet proof vests and sheet iron welded over the back windows and side windows. Each window was outfitted with a sliding cover over its gun-slits. And there were two streamlined 7.62-mm guns bolted on the van's roof, trained downward for a convergent cone of fire.

Link pointed to the west. "See there, man? The ravine ends about four hundred yards out that way, and the ground looks passable. We could circle her."

"They're probably prepared for that too."

"I don't see anything on the bridge."

"They don't want us to. They might simply have undermined it. But I figure there're mines. . . . Let's go in for a closer look."

He eased the van slowly forward, both men straining their eyes to see into the ravine.

The ravine had once been a road, which was now washed out or, farther down, filled in with rubble. The metal guardrails of the overpass had once been painted white. There were a few patches of white left; the rest was rusted, twisted out by crashes, dented by bullet holes. The roadbed was potholed but intact. And ominously deserted.

The sides of the ravine sloped steeply down at a

thirty-five degree angle from the road. Steep—but just maybe . . .

Traveler grinned to himself, and moved the van forward another ten feet. They were only forty feet from the edge.

Traveler stopped the van and said, "Get in back, Link."

Link had learned not to argue with Traveler in emergencies. He climbed in back. Traveler put the van in park and moved over to the passenger seat. "Now take the wheel," Traveler said.

Link got behind the wheel. Traveler got out of the van, carrying the AR15. "That your solution, man?" Link said in mock protest. "Send the poor dumb colored servant in to get his ass blown off while you sneak out the back way?"

Traveler laughed. "I'll be going with you." He bent down and reached under the van, pulled an extendable running board out from under the passenger side door. "Just keep a close lookout." He opened the firing slit on the window and then quietly shut the door, stood on the running board, holding onto the handle with his left hand, the AR15 in his right. "Okay, ease her forward right to the edge of the bridge," Traveler said through the slit in the window.

The sun still burned hot, though it was tinged bloody at the horizon; the door's metal burned under his hand. The ravine came nearer, nearer.

They pulled up closer to the overpass than Traveler would have thought possible without sustaining fire. But still no reaction from his presumed ambushers. Maybe he'd been wrong after all.

"Okay, hold it," he hissed through the window at Link.

The van pulled up four feet short of the bridge. That'd give them just enough room.

"There's a pistol by the steering column, under the dash," Traveler told him. "Grab it, keep it handy. You're probably gonna have to drive and shoot too. . . . Now hold on. . . ."

He eased off the running board, went down on his hands and knees, and crawled belly-down under the van. He could smell its petroleum breath, feel its engine heat just overhead. He reached the left front wheel and looked past it, down into the ravine. From here he had a clear view of the bed of the ravine.

There were two vehicles; one was a long, low flatbed trailer pulled by a converted Mack semi-tractor. The other was a VW Rabbit with its upper sedan section cut away, crudely amputated into a convertible, its sporty yellow paint literally shot to hell—pocked with bullet holes.

There was a 20-mm cannon mounted on the flatbed truck, with its muzzle pointed at the overpass.

"Holy shit," Traveler muttered. "Where the hell did they get that?"

The cannon looked as if it had been pried and cut from a tank mounting, then mounted on the flatbed with crude strut-weldings and chains. There was a crate of shells beside the cannon and two roadrat gunners.

Roadrats. Tribes of half-cracked road pirates, bloodthirsty, inclined to torture, driven mad by the loss of the world as it had been. Only a fortresslike inner character had prevented Traveler from becoming a roadrat himself. It was seductive, in a way.

13

Become a roadrat, and it didn't hurt to be human anymore. Because you *weren't* human anymore.

The two grimy men on the flatbed were typical roadrats. The gunner wore a vest of metal plates held together with wire; two-inch nails had been soldered to the plates so they bristled with points; a dried human finger hung on an earring wire. His head was shaved in checker patches. The gunner's aide looked like a junkyard samurai; he'd put together a rough semblance of a samurai's outfit from strips of leather, chain mail made from bicycle chains wired together, and flattened tin cans. He'd deliberately scarred his face with some crude knife; lightning bolt scars ran up both his cheeks and across his exposed pectorals. He chuckled insanely to himself now and then.

There were two more sitting in the car, smoking smashweed, getting more stoned by the second. One with mirrors carried a crossbow and the other one toted a sawed-off shotgun. There were three more roadrats down at the other end of the gully, beyond the overpass; they were armed with a light rifle and a bazooka. The bazooka was dangerous. Where were they getting the hardware? Traveler wondered. There'd been an "Army" convoy through the area—he'd seen the characteristic jeep tracks more than once. Maybe some big group of roadrats had bushwhacked the convoy, and this bunch had gotten away with a share of the hardcore killing goodies.

Traveler didn't feel bad about that. The gangsters who called themselves "Army" didn't have much relation to the real U.S. Army. Traveler was an ex-military careerist. He still had strong feelings about it.

And he wasn't sure who disgusted him more, roadrats

14

or the Army Glory Boys. He did, though, wish that the Glory Boys would quit "donating"so many guns to the roadrats of the world.

Traveler ducked back, as the roadrats looked up at the Meat Wagon. The two in the car got out and moved into firing position. The one with the shotgun wore a headdress of automobile side mirrors, five of them flashing over his head. Maybe that was the gleam Traveler had seen.

Traveler backed up, under the van, wormed back out onto the right side of the van. He got up, stood on the running board—and was looking into the muzzle of a Colt .45.

"Jesus Christ, man! It's you!" Link said. "Christ, Traveler, I almost blew you away!" He lowered the gun.

"Back up about twenty feet," Traveler said.

Link put the car into reverse and backed up. He stopped twenty feet back and looked questioningly at Traveler.

"You won't believe this," Traveler said, "but they got some kind of 20-mm cannon on a truck. We're going past it. It'll take them awhile to get it turned around to point our way . . .I hope."

"Just what you proposing to do?"

"Head for the ravine. Cut left about thirty degrees from the bridge."

"Man, you aren't planning to—"

"They'll never expect it! Do it!"

"It's your car, man." Link put the car in gear, swung left, and stepped on the gas. The van surged ahead. Traveler hung on, the AR15 in his right hand.

The van reached the edge of the ravine.

Link shouted, "Here we go!" as the van lunged over the brink, into the ravine. For a moment the van hung on the edge, its front wheels suspended in air. Traveler glimpsed the roadrats gaping up at him, just as startled as he'd hoped they'd be. The gunners were already cranking the cannon around on some sort of crude turntable.

And then the Meat Wagon took the plunge, grinding on over the edge and down the steep grade. The thirty-degree angle seemed to the men in the van almost straight down, like they were plunging off a building.

The cannon swung toward them. One of the men hit a switch, and the muzzle roared, belched fire, the slope to the van's left throwing what looked like a half ton of dirt and rock out into the ravine, the van tilting up on its right two wheels with the shock and slamming down again. Traveler hung on desperately, his fingers nearly jerked loose with the wrenching as the van jumped at a second explosion, this one just six feet in front of its ramming wedge. They kept going through a shrapneled cloud of oily smoke. . . . And then they'd reached the floor of the ravine; the Meat Wagon bounced but kept going, rocking, rolling across the gully.

The cannon couldn't reach them at this angle, but the four roadrats were running toward him, raising their weapons, two from one side of the van and two from the other. The two from the cannon were raising home-made pistols and spears. The homemade pistols were made from pipes; they were enlarged versions of the old zip gun. Like a zip gun, they weren't much for accuracy. Both shots missed him, smacking sloppily into the van's hide to Traveler's right. Traveler braced the AR15 on his hip, tilted it out at right angles from

16

him, and squeezed off two bursts, raking into the two roadrats just ten feet off. The cannoneers were blasted off their feet, jerking with the impact of the slugs, spears spinning like thrown parade batons from their hands.

And then the Meat Wagon reached the opposite slope. "Gun it for all she's worth, Link!" Traveler shouted.

Link downshifted to third when he got to the slope, and down to second when they began to climb it.

But the van slowed, began to slide back.

And Link was set upon by the two on the other side. And Traveler saw the three others running down the ravine toward them, just twenty yards off, the third one carrying the bazooka.

"Four-wheel drive, Link!" Traveler shouted, thinking, I forgot to tell him before, dammit, we're fucked—

And then Link kicked in the four-wheel and shifted down into first, and the Meat Wagon began to climb, grinding its way up the steep slope at an angle, the wheels digging for purchase, spitting out dirt at Traveler's ankles.

Link was firing through the left-hand side window at the two road-thugs trying to climb onto the van, using the pistol with one hand and fighting the steering wheel with the other. The man with the shotgun screamed and fell back. The one with the crossbow got a bolt off, shot it through the window—it swished past him and smashed itself on the metal over the window beside Traveler.

The roadrat clung to the window, shrieking crazily, trying to stab through at Link with a bayonet; he managed to cut a shallow rift in Link's cheek. Link twisted away from the knife and fired point-blank through the

17

slit into the roadrat's hate-twisted face, twice; the bullets smashed upward through the roof of the man's mouth, out the top of his head, and through the auto mirrors on his headdress, mixing blood and bone with shattered mirror glass.

Traveler had worries of his own. The van was only halfway up the slope. Another forty feet to the crest. The three roadrats were setting up the bazooka on the floor of the gully, one of them propping it on his shoulder, another loading a shell into it. The third was raising his rifle.

"Come on, Link, dammit, step on it!" Traveler shouted.

"I'm giving it all she's got!" Link shouted.

The Meat Wagon nosed upward, its engine complaining, the exhaust spewing black smoke, steam whining from the radiator, the wheels slipping now and then, the van threatening to slide back. . . .

The bazooka was swiveling to home in on them. . . .

Traveler swore, and shouted, "Meet you up top!"

And leaped off the van onto the slope, firing, shouting, "You fuck up my van with that thing, you better pray you die quick right here and now!"

Traveler rolled down the slope, hit the bottom with bullets making little spires in the dirt around him. He jumped to his feet, snapped the AR15 to his shoulder. A rifle slug ripped away fabric at his right hip, drew a red line across his flesh. And then the AR15 leaped in his hands as he squeezed off the rest of his clip, spurting three-round bursts into the three roadrats and directly into the mouth of the bazooka.

One of Traveler's rounds found its way into the bazooka's muzzle and touched off the shell; the pipelike weapon blew, becoming a thing of viciously ripping shrapnel and roiling fire, reducing the man who held it to a cloud of bloody confetti and blowing the head right off the shoulders of the man who stood behind. The rifleman had fallen with a slug in the shoulder; but he got to his feet bellowing the roadrat cry of suicidal fury and ran hard at Traveler, his waist-length blue-dyed hair streaming out behind him, the rifle abandoned, a knife in his good hand.

Traveler fumbled for another clip—and realized he didn't have one on him. They were in the van. He looked up the slope. The Meat Wagon was just reaching the crest, tilting over onto the flat land. He looked back at the oncoming roadrat—and the man was almost on top of him, howling like a banshee out of hell, his mouth foaming and his eyes pinpoints, his wounded limb swinging dead meat at his side, a bayonet flashing in an arc down at Traveler's head.

Traveler sidestepped and brought the AR15's barrel down on the back of the man's head as the roadrat went by. He felt bone crack sickeningly under the improvised club. The man fell on his face and lay still, blood spurting from the back of his head.

Traveler turned away. He heard a sound behind him, looked over his shoulder, and flung himself aside as the roadrat he'd thought dead lunged at him, slashing with the bayonet. The steel blade ripped at Traveler's flak vest and caught there. Traveler twisted away, and the knife came out of the man's hand. The roadrat was on his hands and knees, snapping his teeth at Traveler's leg, and Traveler realized that this one had the "Killer's plague," the secondary rabies that the Soviets had used as one of their biological warfare agents. The killer's plague took a long time to kill. It made men into human time bombs. One moment they'd seem normal, the next they'd be raving maniacs, triggered by stress. The Soviets had intended it as a weapon of sabotage; sicken a serviceman with secondary rabies and he seems fine— but under pressure he snaps and will turn your operations room into a homicidal maniac's heaven.

Don't let him bite you! Traveler thought, his gut twisting in terror. He wasn't afraid of dying. But dying in madness . . .

He twisted away from the slavering jaws and brought the rifle barrel a second time, hard, down on the man's head.

Blood and brains flew—and Traveler leaped to avoid them.

This time the poor bastard was really dead.

Traveler wiped his gun off carefully on another corpse's clothes, and then trudged up the hill. He was almost at the top when he heard a shout, an engine revving, and two gunshots.

He clawed up over the brink and onto the flat land, and saw Link, outside the van, crouched half behind the door, firing at two more roadrats riding at him on a three-wheel motorcycle. They were both almost naked, wearing leather loincloths, and painted red. One of Link's rounds blew out the front wheel of the bike, and it pitched over, spuming dust and stalling. The roadrats scrambled to their feet and, twenty feet from the van, kept coming, focused on Link, spears in their hands. One of them jerked a homemade one-shot gun from his waistband and ran up to fire it at Link.

Link raised his pistol, but the slide was locked open—empty.

He tossed it into the van and drew a knife.

Traveler ran in from the side, grabbed the gun arm of the savage with the homemade and twisted it back to point at the gunman's mouth just as he squeezed the trigger. The round detonated, and the man's head flew to bloody fragments. Link was up taking on the other, ducking under the spear to stick his long knife under-handed up under the roadrat's rib cage, twisting, cutting his heart neatly in two. The man went limp on Link's arm, and Link let the body fall into the dust.

They stood staring at the corpses. "Where'd these two come from?" Traveler asked.

"Guess they were posted up here in case we got past the ravine," Link said.

Traveler nodded. He turned away and said, "Drift ought to be down the road a short piece. Let's get there and get a drink, get cleaned up. It's gettin' dark. There's probably more around. They hang out around the fringes of the settlements."

Link nodded. They got in, Traveler driving, and drove into the thickening dusk.

And Traveler thought: And we never wonder why they do it, why they want to kill us. Because now the world shows its true colors.

2

The Golden Fleece

It was the closest thing to a real bar in the western half of the North American continent. It was called The Fallout Shelter, and it was in a deep basement room in the very heart of the scrofulous shantytown settlement called Drift, a desert crossroads somewhere in what had once been Nevada. Drift, like Dante's Inferno, was built more or less in circles, and like Hades, it got meaner the nearer to the center you went. The Fallout Shelter was the hardcore of meanness in Drift.

Which was why there was a fellow sitting on a barrel behind the makeshift bar, holding a shotgun. He just sat there, hour after hour, cradling that 12-gauge, waiting for trouble, keeping an eye on strangers.

For the most part there were nothing *but* strangers in the human infestation called Drift. But some were stranger than others. So when the two new strangers came in, a white guy and a tall black guy, fresh from the road, they attracted some attention. Heads turned along the plywood bar as the rough men lining the graffiti-splashed walls drinking one of the house's foul brews or smoking that mutant marijuana, smashweed, looked the two strangers up and down.

Some of the men took a second look and then a third because the two were splashed with as much blood as dust. This was new even for the Shelter.

One of the pair was a medium-tall, compact man with a Mt. Rushmore expression and flat blue eyes. His bristly shock of sandy hair was half-tamed by a black headband-folded bandanna. He wore a flight jacket, torn leather driving gloves, jeans, and combat boots, but, beyond the blood, the Heckler and Koch 91 heavy assault rifle he carried really made him stand out. What passed for the town's constabulary usually didn't allow firearms in Drift. Guns were confiscated, given back only when the gunman left. . . . there *were* one or two guys the "marshall" made exceptions for.

Jamaica Jack, looking at the two strangers, turned to Slasher, the bartender, and said, "You know who that is, man? The white guy, that got to be Traveler, man, sure. He's almost the only guy they let into town with a gun, I heard. And I heard he carries a HK91." Jamaica Jack was an aging mulatto in a filthy sleeveless Levi's jacket and dreadlocks. He had a silver ring in his right nostril and a ju-ju bone stuck through the lobe of his left ear. He sucked on a spliff of smashweed and narrowed his yellowed eyes at the man called Traveler as he came to the bar.

With Traveler was a big, *big* black guy, six foot five at least and built like a weight lifter. He wore the remains of a T-shirt and some black leather pants, that were probably shiny once. He had a wide, jack-o'-lantern grin just now, but his eyes were as emotionless as the desert horizon. Or his partner's. He carried an M16 that looked like a toy in his massive hands.

Slasher, the barman, was a grimy Chicano with black teeth and a face ravaged by radiation-burn scars. Fifteen years before, in 1989, he'd been a little too close to Los Angeles when it went up in the nuclear devastation that put most of the world on a less-than-equal footing with the Mojave Desert.

Slasher hooked a blackened thumb at the man with the shotgun behind him and said, "We don't allow no gunplay here."

"These guns aren't for *play*," Traveler said. "They're for keeps. But we don't use 'em if we're not hassled."

Slasher shrugged. "What you havin'?"

"You got someplace we can clean up, I heard."

"Inna back. Quarter gram o' gold or acceptable ammo trade." In the post-World-War-Three world, gold and ammo were the commonest tradable currencies. After that, working machinery, fuel, and food.

Traveler nodded and placed a small pre-weighed bag of gold dust on the counter. The barman opened it and tested it with a small chemical-proofing kit he kept under the bar. He sifted through it to make sure it was uniformly gold. He nodded and gave it to the shotgunner, who put it into a wall safe behind him. To Traveler he said, "Okay, that'll getcha a cleanup and a couple of drinks. You want the cleanup water boiled?"

"Yeah." Traveler knew that whether or not the bathwater had been used before, there was enough disease going around Drift to kill a healthy horse.

The bartender sent a ragged ten-year-old boy into the back to heat up the tubs of water. Then he turned

25

back to Traveler and asked, "That your blood?" He pointed to the bloodstains on Traveler's hands and face and coat.

"Mostly it was runnin' through some roadrats tried to hijack us a few miles north of here."

"They hijacked 'emselves a ride to hell," the black man said, lifting a tin can of brew to his lips.

"You really gonna drink that stuff, Link?" Traveler asked him.

"You hold your nose, it ain't so bad," Link said. He held his nose with one hand, lifted the cup to his mouth with the other, drank, and set the cup down empty. Then, controlling his expression as best he could, he turned to the bartender and asked in a strained voice, "You got a toilet here?"

"In back."

Link ran for it, choking.

Traveler chuckled and said, "I hope the toilet and the bathtub aren't one and the same in this dump."

When they'd cleaned up—*scraped off* would be a better way to put it—Traveler and Link returned to the main room and found it cooking with Drift's night life at its peak. If you could package Drift's night life, and if there were still such things as surgeon generals, the surgeon general would order a warning put on the package: "The Surgeon General has determined that Drift's Night Life is hazardous to your Health."

There were only two fights going on in the room that evening, however.

One of the roadrats had made the mistake of coming into the hot room without a jacket—which revealed that that particular roadrat was a woman.

26

With roadrats, it's hard to tell.

This one in particular was frogfaced, squat, squamous, grimy as the underside of a semi-truck, and her few remaining teeth had been filed to points. She had a crude tattoo of a scorpion down the right side of her face. Women were hard to come by, though, so a group of men approached her hoping for a quickie.

They came in a group because she was a roadrat, and they knew she'd be mean.

"Mean," as it happened, was an understatement, Traveler noted, as he watched the woman use a spike clamped to her elbow to gouge a man's eye out; a second man tried to wrestle her down, and she used her file teeth to do a cookie-cutter number on his throat; the third man she simply flattened with a strong left hook.

"That broad can sure kick some ass," Link said.

Traveler nodded. They drank a little fermented canned fruit cocktail juice, standing with their backs to the wall in the dimness between two scallops of lamplight. The "jack," as the fermented juice was called, wasn't bad, except it tasted like the cans they drank it from.

The mulatto Rasta appeared from nowhere and said, "Sure she kick ass, frien', that's the Spike, queen bitch of the Road Wasps."

"They should make up their mind what species they are," Link said. "Are they rodents or insects or what?"

"Oughta be called Road Pigs," Traveler said.

The town marshall was questioning the bartender about the killing. Having satisfied himself that the killing was some version of "self-defense," he ordered his deputies to tote the bodies out and told the Spike to put on a jacket.

"The hell with that," she rasped. "After tonight I'm

27

gonna cut 'em off an' cauterize the stumps. Fucking tits jus' get inna way innyhow."

"A real charmer," Traveler muttered.

"She's a dyke," Jamaica Jack informed him. "But, them roadrats worship 'er."

The other fight was taking place in a far corner, a tussle over alleged cheating in a dice game. There was a ring of men around the fighters, ignoring the deputies' attempts to break it up. Traveler heard a scream and then one of the men said, "Ah, shit, it's too easy to cut his spine like that." And then the fight was over and the bored watchers drifted away.

Traveler yawned.

A jug band started its thump and whinnying in another corner. A group of raggedy skinheads did a "Hoi! Hoi! Hoi!" slamdance to the beat.

Traveler turned to Link. "I had enough night life."

"We just got here, man. You tired of the comforts of 'civilization' so soon?"

Traveler snorted and said, "See you at the Meat Wagon. I'm leaving first thing in the morning."

Link nodded. Traveler hefted his assault rifle and began to elbow through the crowd. And that's when the old man climbed onto the bar.

Looking up at the old man, Traveler had a funny feeling, a feeling that he usually had just before things flew apart. It felt like he was seeing an omen. An omen of Death. It was beginning here, at this instant, a lethal chain reaction beginning with an old man shouting at the crowd.

"Get the hell off the bar!" the shotgunner said.

"Fuck you!" the old man snarled. "Shoot me if you

28

want—but listen up first! I'm the Old Man in the Hole, and I got uh 'nouncement tuh make!"

The room quieted. They'd heard of the Old Man in the Hole, and looking at him, enough of them recognized him.

He was said to be a prospector who lived in an old mine shaft somewhere out in the desert. He was known for two things: having plenty of gold and having even more meanness. Twelve men had died, it was said, trying to find the whereabouts of his diggings—or trying to waylay the old man on the way.

He was a pallid, blue-lipped old man with yellowing eyes and a corona of white hair and beard all the way around his craggy face. His ancient overalls were dirty beyond belief and falling apart. But the Thompson submachine gun—half a century old—held steadily in his gnarled hands was battered but shiny with oil and ready to cut down any man who tried to stop this speech.

"You all know about my gold!" the old man bellowed. "And gold will still buy goods anywhere in the world! Well, lemme tell you somethin'—I'm gonna give that gold to you! An' I got a little surprise for you—it's aready in bullion! That's cause it wasn't no mine! I found me a vault hidden away in the mountains, and tunneled into it! It's fulla gold bricks! I figure it was owned by old Howard Hughes himself! Now lissen here—I'm gonna give out ten maps to where to find that gold! Right here and now! Whoever gits there first, he gets the gold! And you know *why* I'm givin' it to you?" He howled with laughter and grabbed a bottle off a shelf behind the bar, swigged down a triple hit as the men in the room before him shuffled impatiently. He smashed the bottle against the wall. The heavy behind the bar with the shotgun finally noticed the old man's Thompson and, scowling, said "You ain't supposed to have a gun in here!" As he raised his shotgun to point at the old man's back, Slasher pushed the barrel down and said, "Let the man have his say."

The Old Man in the Hole wiped his mouth, spat, and went on, "I give you these here maps because—*I hate every one of you assholes!*" He roared with laughter, swaying on the bartop, till his eyes teared. "An'—An'—An'—Haw haw!—An' I know if I give you assholes the maps, you'll kill each other gettin' to this treasure! That'll kill off more of you than I ever could! And make fools of you too!"

"We ain't fools enough to chase after gold that don't exist!" someone yelled.

"Oh, it exists, friend!" the old man replied, spraying spittle over the audience in his fervor. "That gold is out there just where I say it is! And here's some proof!" He took a pouch from his waist-rope and opened it. He stuck the Thompson in his armpit, clamped it against his side, and used the freed hand to take ten six-by-four-inch plates of gold out of the pouch. "I made a mold!" he shouted. "The map's on each one of these! Here! Solid gold! Trade it for food—or go for the bullion!"

And, one by one, he tossed the gold plates out into the audience. A roadrat yelped as a sharp-edged spinning gold plate slashed into his cheek and stuck there. He yanked it out and, ignoring the pain, wiped the blood off the gold—if you can ever get blood off gold— and squinted at it. Someone snatched it from him and ran. The roadrat jerked a handmade double-barbed minicrossbow from his coat and shot the thief in the back. There were leather thongs attached to the arrow shafts. He hauled the corpse—still gripping the plate—back to him.

Similar encounters were taking place all over the bar. A riot erupted, and the bar roared as men slammed and smashed and stabbed one an other. The old man roared, too—with laughter.

Link had nabbed one of the plates. Three men looked at him and then at the plate in Link's hand. They were roadrats wearing the plastic yellow jackets of the Road Wasps. They stood six feet away, hemming Link into a corner.

"You give us that map, boy," one of them said, "and maybe we let you live."

As the roadrat spoke, he drew a short-handled jagged-edged scythe from beneath the back of his jacket and flourished it.

The second drew a machete. The third hefted a mace tipped with steel spikes.

Link looked around for Traveler and didn't see him. His M16 was strapped across his back. Before he could get it into firing position, they'd slice him to pieces.

Link shrugged.

"You want it, you got it." He held the sharp-edged plate between thumb and forefinger and threw it like a shuriken at the man in the middle, the one with the machete. The plate sank into the man's right eye. He shrieked and clawed at the gore-spouting wound. The other two turned to grab at the plate, and that give Link the moment he needed. He shrugged the gun off his shoulders, swung it into firing position, pulled the trigger—nothing. It had jammed. Should have cleaned it after that fight on the road.

"Tsk," he said. "Getting sloppy." As the two strug-

31

gling thugs turned back toward him, he reversed the gun and used it like a club, swinging the butt to stove in the skull of the man with the mace—and hoping the plastic would make it through yet another hand-to-hand. The man went down with a sheeplike bleat, the plate clutched in his hand. But the third was swinging the scythe at Link and there just wasn't time to get out of the way—

Thunk.

The scythe-wielder went down; a shuriken, a real four-pointed throwing star this time, stuck deeply between his eyes. Traveler stepped in to scoop up both the gold plate and the shuriken and said, "Let's get before they make me use my gun. Don't wanna waste ammo, and I sure don't want to get all dirty again."

The old man was howling with laughter on the bar. "I'm gonna die!" He was shouting. "I got me a tumor big as a baseball in my gut! So do it and die, boys!" With that enigmatic cry, he opened up on the bar with his Thompson, the ear-shattering pounding of the submachine gun filling the small, smoky room as the long SMG burst made shards of the bottles and sent chunks of wood flying. He turned to open up on the crowd, and then the shotgunner—who'd wisely hidden under the bar—popped up like a jack-in-the-box and let go both barrels of the shotgun into the old man's back, pasting his tumor to the ceiling.

There were a few moments of shocked silence as the old man's almost bisected body pitched into the crowd.

Traveler and Link used that moment of shock to slip out of the room and up the narrow stairs to the street.

Street? A scummed-over alley, with scummed-over

people lying about in it, drunk or simply starving, mumbling to themselves.

As they stepped out onto the street, they heard more gunshots in the room below and screams and shouts of warning and the sounds of glass and furniture being broken.

"The old man sure had a good joke on 'em," Link said.

"I wonder if nine men'll come out of it alive," Traveler muttered. He led the way through the darkened maze of alleys to the main street, lit with guttering torches.

The word would get out, he knew. There would be a lot of competition for those gold plates in Drift. A lot more men would die for them.

He looked at the plate in his hand. The smart thing to do would be to pitch it into the gutter.

Link glanced at him. "If you don't want it, friend, I do."

Traveler passed it to him. "I don't like the odds. And the old man probably booby-trapped the vault."

Link stuck the plate in his back pocket. "Yeah. Guess I'll just go after the gold all alone."

"Guess you will."

"Face all those guys alone. On foot. Just me against nine men, maybe more. Maybe the whole Road Wasps gang. Fine, man. No probs."

Traveler chuckled. "Toss the fucking thing away."

"Are you kidding? No way. I'm tired of living like a rat. With this bullion a man could get to a civilized part of the world. They say there are still places, in the Southern Hemisphere . . ."

Traveler nodded, looking thoughtful.

Yeah. A Traveler could do a lot of traveling with all that bullion. . . . "C'mon, friend," he said, "let's go get ourselves killed."

3

The Road Has Claws

There was a man with an arrow sticking out of his chest dying beside the back door to Traveler's van. He was lying on his back, choking, blood trailing from the corners of his mouth, clutching weakly at the shaft in his chest. The doors of the Meat Wagon were booby-trapped, so that when anyone tried to open it—anyone who didn't know where the hidden release mechanism was—they'd be damn sorry.

"I thought you paid a guy to watch the van," Link said.

"That's him," Traveler said. "Guess the temptation got to be too much."

He bent over the man, his 12-inch combat knife in his hand. If the fool had been alive, he'd have cut his throat. Not out of vindictiveness, but out of pity. Put him out of his misery. There just weren't any doctors left. The booby-trap had saved him the trouble—the man was dead.

Traveler disengaged the booby traps, and he and Link got into the Meat Wagon. They simply stepped over the dead man's body and left it behind. It'd probably fill out some roadrat club's cooking pot—or go to feed some landowner's guard dogs. Nothing went to waste in Drift.

"How you figure to tackle this?" Link asked.

"I'm wide open for ideas," Traveler said, as he put the assault rifle on its rack. He slid behind the wheel and Link took the passenger's seat, literally riding shotgun: he stowed his jammed M16 and rode carrying Traveler's 12-gauge riot shotgun—a pump-action Remington 870.

"We got a full tank of gas an' some extra," Link said. "I say we go for it now. They're gonna be hot on our tail. . . ."

He was looking at the map in the dim light filtering through the window, as Traveler started the van. "Due south along the highway. Then at Skull Rock it veers off into the desert. Says 'dirt road southwest.' "

"Then let's do it." Traveler put the Meat Wagon into gear, and they headed for the checkpoint in the barrier that went all the way around the shantytown.

The Meat Wagon was a compact black van with a short, low snout, sharply raked windshield, and four-wheel drive. It had a Wankel rotary engine under the hood. With its oversized wheels and top speed of 140 mph, it kicked ass even on a dirt road. The rotary engine was ideal for this land of shortage. It would run on anything that burns—gasoline, diesel, vodka, tequila, perfume, kerosene . . . The tank was full of gas—scavenged from an overturned roadrat truck after the fight down the road—and there were four cans sloshing with kerosene in the back. The interior of the van had been gutted, replaced with bulletproof vests, and iron shutters across the windows. Special firing slots were cut into the doors, blocked off by sliding steel covers most of the time, till it was necessary for Traveler to slide those covers back and jam a gun snout through. Chain mail skirts hung rattling over the wheels to deflect stray bullets from the tires. Overhead he'd mounted two 7.62-mm machine guns, all but the muzzles enclosed in a streamlining teardrop of fiber glass. The machine guns were aimed downward, their point of aim converging at a spot in the van's path about forty feet off. Traveler knew all the time, no matter where he was, just where that cone of fire would be.

Traveler knew weapons.

Sixteen years before, before the world war that had chewed away the face of the planet, before the nuclear holocaust that had incinerated Traveler's wife and child, Traveler had been a Special Forces operative in Central America fighting with the contras against the dictatorial Communist regime tyrannizing El Hiagura. And then he and his team—Hill, Orwell, and Margolin— had walked into a trap. The enemy had grabbed the chance to test its new weapon, the yellowdust neurotoxin that had changed Traveler forever, a weapon given them by an American officer playing both ends of that war. It nearly killed him—but he survived and came to his senses in an American military hospital. The antitoxin they gave him eventually cured him . . . except for certain side effects. It had somehow altered his neurosystem, giving him something akin to a sixth sense, and making the other five weirdly acute. It also left him a little bit prone to paranoia, giving him an edge of craziness that was maybe the only reason he'd survived so long, despite the odds against him.

He'd stumbled across Orwell—but what about Hill and Margolin? They'd been sent to separate hospitals, and after the war—the goddamn forty-five-minute war, that was no real war at all, really a mutual fire storm of butchery—after that, he'd lost them. But he knew they were out there, somewhere. Alive. He could sense it. There'd been an animalistic psychic bond between the four fighting men. And if they'd died, he'd have felt it. . . .

Thinking these things, remembering, Traveler drove through the checkpoint and out onto the highway, into the star-roofed darkness of the Mojave Desert.

They drove in shifts. It was close to the end of Link's second shift, just at the brink of dawn, that Traveler woke, sensing something was wrong.

There was a sound that shouldn't be there.

"Sounds like bikers," Traveler said, sitting up. "Lots of them."

"You havin' a dream, man," Link said. "I don't hear nothing."

"You will," Traveler said, checking the load on the Remington 870. "It's my turn at the wheel. You take this."

Traveler handed the weapon to Link as they quickly exchanged positions, Traveler deftly climbing into the driver's seat as Link jumped out and bolted around the front of the Meat Wagon. Link barely had time to close the door before the Meat Wagon roared down the highway.

Looking back through the rearview slit in the back-door shielding, Link saw five headlights. "You're spooky, man. Yeah, there they are moving up on us. Look like outriders for the Road Wasps horde. Great. They probably lookin' for me, after that little spot of fun 'n' games with their people."

"Yeah?" Traveler said. "I guess you want to do the heroic thing and let me leave you on the road for them to find so I can get away free."

"Traveler, man, your sense of humor is too *weird*."

Traveler chuckled. "I guess that means we're just going to have to do something about these assholes before they do something about *us*."

The dawn was coming on strong now, making the sky look like metal going from red to white hot at the horizon. There was just enough light . . .

"If I remember right, there's a turnoff around the next bend," Traveler said. "Let's see if they follow us through the gulch."

He stomped the gas pedal, and the van snorted, then roared as it picked up speed, the tail end breaking loose in a controlled slide as he took the sharp bend. Just around the bend, out of sight from their pursuers, there was a dirt side road leading off to the right, west. It wasn't the road indicated by the map, so if the bikers followed him here instead of barging on, they were interested in more than just a race for the treasure. They were into killing off the competition first.

Traveler swung hard onto the road and switched into four-wheel drive as they bounced and jolted over the rutted earth. Up ahead the road sank between two high outcroppings of rock, marking the opening of a gulch. Traveler had camped there once.

He drove into the gulch with Link looking at him sidelong, wondering if he were in his right mind.

"They following right behind, man," Link said, from the back. "They saw our dust."

"That's what I counted on," Traveler said.

"Fine situation," Link said. "I'm being chased by crazy men, and I'm riding in a car driven by a crazy man."

"I doubt they're after you," Traveler said. "You in particular. I figure the Spike decided to send her crew to wipe out the competition. She must've got one of those maps. Hold on!"

And he swerved hard right as he passed out of the gulch, bringing the Meat Wagon to a shuddering halt behind a stack of reddish boulders. He did a U-turn, got back on the road, and began to back up so that he was just over the crown of the low hill that rose at this end of the gulch; here he'd be invisible from riders in the gulch till they were nearly on top of him.

The gulch acted as a funnel. The road narrowed to pass between the sandstone bluffs. Coming out of the gulch, the riders would have to ride close together, and the stone enclosures would prevent them from out-flanking him.

And he was just fifty feet from the point where they'd come out of the gulch. . . .

He saw a headlight glow at the top of the hill. He moved forward ten feet, to the top, and there they were, forty feet below, just emerging from the gulch—and driving directly into his cone of fire. Coming two by two. Link had missed one—there were *six* Road Wasps, their bikes tricked out with spikes and gouging hooks on the side; each bike had a yellow-and-black-striped paint job and a sort of barbed horn out front, the stinger, thrusting from the center of the handlebars.

"Those wasps fly backwards," Link said. Traveler pressed the fire button mounted on his steering wheel and backed up slowly, sweeping the wheel left and right to cover the whole road.

The two big machine guns overhead were rattling murderously, spitting muzzle flash and slugs. The clatter of disintegrating links and spent cases drumming on the roof was like hail. The convergent automatic weapon fire caught the two lead bikers squarely in the chests, splitting them open and knocking them off their bikes at the same time, smashing them backwards into the front wheels of the two bikes following, whose riders were in turn pitched off their bikes headfirst at impact. The last two riders split up to ride around the carnage, almost scraping the rocks to either side, coming one on each side of the Meat Wagon, riding hard. The one on the left had a shotgun mounted on the handlebars above the stinger. He swiveled it on its mount to point at the van's windshield. But Traveler was already accelerating forward, unexpectedly burning rubber to run between the two bikes, so that the shotgun blast missed the windshield and smacked into the van's metal side damaging nothing but the paint. The other biker fired a crossbow arrow through the open window—the shaft sang by just under Traveler's chin, so close its fletch burned the skin of his throat, splintering itself against the doorframe.

Traveler pulled up short of the burning wreckage of the four fallen bikes and shouted, "Link—!"

But the command wasn't necessary. Link had snatched his M16 from the front rack and dived back to poke it through the rear firing slit. As the two bikers came around for another pass, he met them head on with two short bursts, catching one in the mouth, mixing his teeth with his brains and knocking him off his bike; the other screamed as four rounds ripped open his sternum, splitting his breastbone in two. He clung spasmodically to the bike and rode it, a corpse rider, head on into the rear of the van. The Meat Wagon lurched with the impact, but the only real damage was done to the bike which rebounded, crumpled and fluttering with fire.

Traveler and Link got out, carrying a coil of rope. They went over the bodies for ammo, weapons, anything useful. Then Traveler used the rope to tie the six bodies to the back of the van, like fish on a string, each corpse lashed on at an ankle. He got into the van and calmly drove back to the road, the dead roadrats bumping along behind. In the passenger seat now, Link looked hard at Traveler, trying to figure him out. But he knew Traveler didn't like to be asked a lot of questions. So he shrugged and worked on clearing his M16.

They swung onto the main road. No sign of the rest of the roadrat horde. They had already passed on, up ahead.

Traveler smiled grimly and shifted gears, gunned the van to top speed.

By the time they caught up with the bulk of the Road Wasps—four on bikes and seven in the souped-up wrecks that passed for cars among roadrats—the dead bodies jouncing and twirling and tangling behind the Meat Wagon were flayed, bloodied almost beyond recognition. But the gang colors were still visible on their jackets. The crushed bodies left smudges of blood on the road behind the van.

"Christ," Link muttered, "no wonder you call it the Meat Wagon."

Traveler sprayed a short warning burst up the middle of the road as he caught up with the Wasps' road fleet. Instinctively, the horde parted, moving out of his fire-path, and he gunned up the middle, passed them, and kept going.

"Cut the rope, man," Traveler said.

Link climbed into the back, opened the back door, and used his belt knife to slashed the rope away.

Traveler zigzagged the van just before the rope parted, so the six bodies were spread out over the width of the road.

The horde ground to a stop before the grisly barrier, and in his side mirror Traveler could see the queen of the Wasps, the Spike, getting out of an awning-covered car, a motorized palanquin, to inspect the bodies. He saw her jump up and down with rage.

"Maybe they'll think twice before they mess with us again," Traveler said.

"Or maybe they'll try twice as hard, twice as pissed now," Link said as he crawled up front.

Traveler shrugged.

Link tried to figure out how to get some sleep.

4

Take a Right at Death

Skull Rock was roughly shaped like a skull, it was true, and at some point it had been chiseled to give it two hollow eye sockets. But that wasn't really why it was called Skull Rock. It was because the road tribe of cannibals that had set it up there had used hot tar to glue hundreds of human skulls to it, crusting it all the way around like barnacles. A skull covered with skulls, ten feet high, staring yellowish and gray from the side of the road. No one knew whether they were giving warning or bragging.

"Cannibals, huh?" Link said. "They still around?"

"You bet your ass."

"That's exactly what I'm betting. Or maybe my skull."

They swung off the road to the right, onto the sparse track beside the skull. Heading southwest.

It was almost noon. Somewhere behind them the Road Wasps were buzzing angrily up the road. Maybe a mile behind. . . . And there were others, Traveler suspected. Maybe out in the desert, maybe ahead, maybe behind. Going for the gold.

There was a range of sawtooth hills up ahead, a washed-out blue against the gray-blue of the sky. The yellowish desert was patched with sage and tumbleweed, notched by crevices, studded with boulders. Here and there a wiry tree eked out a thirsty existence.

"Don't look like the road was recently traveled," Link said.

Traveler nodded. Drifts of sand snaked across the road every few hundred feet. Tumbleweed brushed under the Meat Wagon as they ground along through the desert. The heat was building, and Traveler had slid back the iron side windows despite the danger of roadside snipers.

Link swore, coughing, as dust came in his window, blowing directly into his face. He tied a bandanna over his mouth so he looked like the outlaws who'd robbed stagecoaches on this road more than a century before, and asked, "Hey, Traveler, uh—you mind if I ask you a personal question?"

"Yah. I do."

"I'm gonna ask anyway. You don't have to answer."

"Damn right, I don't."

"I saw some pictures in that crate you took the rope out of. Bunch of guys in uniform. That the outfit you were with in Central America?"

Traveler hesitated. Then he shrugged. "Yeah. I found one of 'em. The black guy, Orwell. I hope to see him, if I get where I'm going."

Him, and Jan. Something tightened in Traveler's gut when he thought of Jan, American Indian warrior woman he'd fought beside and lain beside, months before.

46

"You think the others are alive?" Link asked.

"Yeah, they're alive . . . I think. I'd know if they died. I'd feel it." He shrugged again. "I think Hill and Margolin are alive out there, somewhere. They may be crazy from the dose we got. . . ."

"What's that?"

"NT77. Neurotoxin 77—a nerve gas that overloads up your senses—"

"No, I mean: What's *that*?" Link pointed off to their left.

Traveler looked. Something was making a long horizontal plume of dust as it ran parallel to them, about a hundred fifty yards off. "A car. Hard to make out through the dust." Whatever it was, it was low to the ground and built roughly on the lines of an old dragstrip dragster, long and stripped down, its wheels rising higher than the driver's head. Traveler thought he made out two figures, side by side in the modified dragster. Somebody else after the gold.

The dragster veered abruptly, cutting across the desert to intersect their path, swerving to avoid boulders, but moving like a streak.

"Faster than we'll ever be," Link muttered.

The dragster cut across the road ahead of them, not forty feet off. Traveler glimpsed a muzzle flashing in the sun below the silhouette of a man—and then the Meat Wagon's windshield starred with a bullet hole as the man riding shotgun in the dragster took a potshot at them.

Traveler and Link both instinctively ducked. When they looked up again, the car was gone, just a receding glint of metal in a cloud of dust to the west.

"You get the feeling they trying to tell us something?" Link said.

Traveler nodded. "Whatever they have to say I don't want to hear. You know how long it'll take me to get a new windshield."

"Probably getting back on the road way ahead of us. Maybe they got enough of a lead in that thing we're wasting our time."

Traveler shook his head. "It's fast, but the countryside's too rugged for a machine like that. And if the road don't get 'em, the cannibals will."

"I figure we maybe outdistanced these cannibals. . . ."

"Uh-uh. Look at that!"

Up ahead the ground rose to a low ridge, the road running through a notch at the ridge's top edge. The ridgetop was alive. It was alive with the silhouettes of men. And coming down the road at them, rolled at them with levers, were three boulders, each stone big as the Meat Wagon.

"Holy shit!" Link blurted.

The enormous gray boulders came bouncing down like hungry things leaping after prey, roughly following the road, splashing dust at each point of impact, shaking the ground with their coming, dislodging other rocks that rolled down like minions beside them.

Traveler looked hard at the nearest boulder's trajectory, saw that it was going to bounce off an outcropping before reaching him. He drove hard at the outcropping, braking just as he reached it. The boulder struck and bounded over the van, thumping down hard behind it; the other two rolled to either side of the outcropping, like a wake parting around a prow, and thundered harmlessly by.

The rumbling died down. A wall of dust billowed by, swallowing the Meat Wagon.

A few smaller rocks rattled past. Then there was silence.

"Now what?" Link asked rhetorically.

"Now we play some music," Traveler said.

Link looked at him, startled. "What?"

Traveler found an old cassette he'd scavenged from a ruin and shoved it into the player in his glove compartment. He reached behind his seat and lifted out the two-foot wooden speaker cabinet, wedged it into the window to his left. Then he backed up the van, got back onto the road, and started up the hill. He shifted gears for a hill, and said, "Hit the play button and turn the volume all the way up."

Link started the tape and turned up the volume.

Iggy and the Stooges' "Search & Destroy," from the early seventies. LP *Raw Power* thundered out over the hillside. Early punk metal-rock. The raw stuff. At this volume, coming like a shriek of supernatural warning out of the Meat Wagon—with its clusters of rusty spikes on its bumpers and fenders, its ramming wedge welded onto the front end, its topside machine guns gleaming lethally in the sun . . .

The new savages backed up, confused, uncertain, frightened by the air-raid-siren shriek of the electric guitar blasting from the tape deck.

Link laughed, and Traveler smiled grimly as the savages panicked, driven back by nothing more than sound. "It won't hold them long," Traveler said, when they'd reached the ridgetop. Below them, in a shallow, arid valley between two ridges, was a ghost town, dun-colored, beginning to crumble into the desert around it, six rows of rickety wooden buildings with false fronts, boarded-over windows, tumbleweed-choked streets.

"Maybe that's where the cannibals hole up," Link said.

"No," Traveler said, as they started down the ridge. "They live out in the open, or in caves. They're superstitious about places like that. . . . Hell, here they come!"

The cannibals were rushing them from the sides, clothed only in body paints.

"They're just kids!" Link burst out.

"Teenagers mostly. Children orphaned by the war and gone savage. You're looking at *Lord of the Flies* time."

Having decided that the van was just another human artifact and nothing demonic—their second mistake—the children's crusade rushed in with suicidal abandon.

Nightmarish in a cloud of yellow dust, youthful faces brutalized by exposure and atavism and filth, the young cannibals leaped onto the Meat Wagon; they were clinging to the roof and the metal rim over the windshield, standing on the ramming wedge with their faces pressed to the windshield glass, or clawing madly through the side windows. The men in the van had no choice: it was time to fight or die.

Traveler reached under the dashboard, found the holster wired there, and drew a Colt Government Model Mark IV .45 pistol. Without hesitation he jammed it into a snarling face at the window slit on his left and pulled the trigger. He heard a yelp and out of the corner of his eye saw something fall away but kept his eyes on the road.

Link had grabbed one of the cannibal's gutting hooks as it came in through the side window. It was shaped like a pike, with a hook and a spike both, made of scavenged scrap metal, jagged and rusty, held together with twisted wire. The whole thing was less than four feet long.

A mohawk-headed, blue-painted road cannibal was trying to force his way through the window. He had snaggled yellow teeth—and clamped in those teeth was a hunk of bloody red meat. The road cannibals believed that, when attacking an enemy, keep the raw meat of another enemy in your mouth, and you'll win.

The pike wasn't doing this kid much good. Link jammed the spike into the punk's face and twisted. The kid fell off the van, dying. Another climbed halfway through the window before Link caught him through the throat with the hook, ripped counterclockwise, spraying the interior of the van with blood.

"Hey, don't mess up my car, bro," Traveler said. "Ruin my upholstery."

Link shoved the dying cannibal out and finally slid the metal window shutter home. It had taken less than three minutes since they first saw the rocks rolling down the hill at them.

Traveler yanked the van from side to side with vicious jerks of the steering wheel, trying to dislodge the others; one of them fell, was impaled on the bumper spikes, stuck there writhing, spewing blood, clawing at the rusty protrusions at his belly; another fell onto the ramming wedge, tumbled off, screamed once before the Meat Wagon's big cheaters ground over him.

A third, standing on the rammer and clinging to the roof with one hand, used his other hand to smash a short-pike into the windshield where the bullet hole had starred it, widening the crack, smashing through—

"Shit!" Traveler snarled. "I just put that glass in!"

He stuck the muzzle of the Colt through the hole in the glass and squeezed off a round, directly into the blue-faced road cannibal's foaming mouth. Teeth and cartilage and blood spattered the glass, and the cannibal fell under the wheels. The Meat Wagon fairly jumped onto and over the body, as if expressing its anger at the damage done to it, crunching the cannibal beneath and leaving the wreckage contemptuously behind.

In the hubbub from the attackers on the front of the van, they hadn't heard the noise made by the cannibal climbing in the back. They didn't know he was there till his pike slashed past Link's ear, gouging a bloody rift in the skin of his neck. The pike would have split Link's head open if Traveler hadn't swerved, making the cannibal miss—purely by chance.

Link grabbed the haft of the pike and wrenched it away. The road cannibal clawed at his face with repulsively unclean, overgrown nails—and then rebounded from the inner wall of the van as Traveler put a .45 round through the side of his head, looking up from the road for a split second to fire, looking back at the road before the brain-splashed cannibal had fallen.

"Sneaky sons of bitches," Link grumbled, as he improvised a bandage over his wound. Then he checked the rest of the van. The other cannibals had been shaken off—except for the one clinging to the roof. Traveler slammed on the brakes, jerking the savage forward to fall clawing half down the front, hugging the muzzles of the machine guns to its chest as he tried to clamber back up top.

"May I?" Link asked.

"Be my guest," Traveler said.

Link reached over and pressed the fire button on the steering column. The 7.62-mm guns blasted a short burst that—at point-blank range—blew the cannibal off the van, sending him flying twenty feet to the front. The big machine gun rounds at point-blank range had blown a hole so big in his chest you could see the rocks in the road through the hole as he fell lifeless onto his back. They drove by him and left road cannibal territory behind.

The road wound around another bend and then straightened as it fed into the flatland between the ridges. Fifty yards ahead was the snaggly graveyard that held the forgotten founders of the old ghost town. Above the ghost town, above the far ridge, rose the blue sawtooth hills, an arm of the Sierras, blue as the skin of a dead man. The Deathgate Hills. . . .

Looking at the map, Link said, "We go on straight through the ghost town, over the next ridge, across Cattle Ivory Flats, and up into the hills at the Blasted Pine. The vault is somewhere in those hills."

"We're gonna have to stop here, let the engine cool," Traveler said, looking at the gauges. "She's overheating. Maybe find some water here."

"Maybe find something else," Link said. "I got a feeling we won't be alone in this ghost town."

Grinning in death, the corpse in the back of the van rode with them to the town.

5

A Ghost Town
Haunted by the Living

They left the corpses of two cannibals in the middle of the road at the entrance to the town beside a broken-down sign that, faded, still held the town's name: *Hope Chest.*

Link arranged one of the bodies so it was sitting up against the signpost, staring glassily back along the trail, one arm propped on an upraised knee, the fingers of the hand bent back to give a one-finger salute to whoever came along behind. A crow landed on the corpse's cracked forehead and began to peck the still-oozing brains out of the smashed skull.

Link and Traveler drove on into town and parked in the shade of the half-fallen Blacksmith shop.

The Colt .45 on his hip, the AR15 in his arms, Traveler got out and looked up and down the street. Link, carrying the shotgun, came to stand behind him.

"Damn, it's quiet," Link said.

Traveler nodded. It was eerily, scarily quiet.

The row of buildings across the street stood like weathered tombstones, waiting only for the casual kick of a vandal before they collapsed into dust and splinters. What windows weren't boarded over were gaping and spider-webbed.

"Set of tire tracks in the street," Link said. "And they ain't ours. Looks like the dragster."

"Yeah. . . . There's water here, somewhere," Traveler said.

"How do you know?"

"I can smell it," Traveler said flatly, as if it should be obvious.

"Man, you're better than a good dog when it comes to finding things. Think you can find me a beer?"

Traveler ignored the gibe. "We'll wait here, let the car cool. You keep an eye on it; I'll check out the town, locate the water."

"You got it."

He felt exposed walking down the middle of the street. The lifeless buildings to either side might not be so lifeless. They might be like zombies—dead, but with something evil in them, living on.

There *was* someone there. Watching him. He could feel it.

He checked the clip on the AR15. It was full. But he had only one clip left.

He walked down the middle of the road, then moved off to slip between two buildings, feeling less vulnerable as he walked down a narrow alley between the rows of half-fallen houses. All the time he followed the scent of water. . . .

There it was. At the edge of town.

An old well with an ancient, rusty hand pump. He could see it framed by the end of the alley. The shadows were growing long and deepening. The afternoon was wearing on.

He stepped out of the alley and into the yellow-dust corral area between a ramshackle barn and a fallen-in livery stable. He paused, listening. There it was again—a furtive movement to his left.

He swung the rifle around—and a startled lizard looked at him in alarm, then darted into the shadows of the stable.

Just a lizard.

But something else was there. . . .

He sensed it now, a presence in the stable. Standing stone-motionless, he could hear the faint intake of a breath being drawn. And a click.

He threw himself down, and the bullets kicked up the dust where he'd been standing a moment before. The automatic weapon burst echoed around the ghost town. A crow was startled into flight, flapped cawing noisily in a circle overhead, as Traveler leaped up and dodged back into the alley. Another spray of gunfire tore splintery hunks from the wooden corner of the building he dodged behind.

His heart pounding, he spun around, alerted by a noise behind, glimpsed a silhouette at the other end of the alley. He squeezed off a three-round burst at the silhouette and threw himself flat as the answering fire whined overhead. The silhouette dodged back into a sagging doorway.

"Shit," Traveler muttered.

He was caught between two of them. Maybe more. They'd waited here, in ambush, knowing that anyone who drove in across the dusty flats would be coming for the water.

He stood—and threw himself flat against the wall. Another burst from down the alley licked at him with muzzle flash and smashed through the wall across from him. He dodged back out into the corral area and zigzagged to the left, flattening himself beside the skewed doorway of the stable.

Another muzzle flash—this time from the darkness of the barn across the corral. He had the AR15 diagonally across his chest, and that saved him: a bullet kicked off the barrel, knocking the gun against him, banging him against the wall, kicking the air out of his chest; the round ricocheted off into the dirt. The front sight was dented but the gun was still functional, and gasping, Traveler used it to toss off another three-round burst at the barn.

He heard footsteps in the alley to one side and someone moving up behind him in the stable. He was trapped.

And then the Meat Wagon barreled around the stable from the left, its topside guns hammering at the barn, scouring the interior with hot lead. Someone screamed and fell, inside. The Meat Wagon swung around in the middle of the corral and came about to hammer at the stable. Bullets spanged off its armor from the alley.

Traveler knew the shooter in the alley would be focusing his attention on the van. He moved to the alley and locked onto the outline at the other end, firing into the man-shadow. The man flung up his arms and fell back, his silhouette permanently altered by three rounds to and through the top of his head.

There was the sound of glass breaking and running

feet from behind. Whoever was in the stable had broken a window and taken it on the lam out the back way.

Link pulled up beside Traveler and said, "Taxi, mister?"

Traveler grinned. "You got good instincts, Link. Thanks."

"Just good ears, man. I heard all that gunfire and somethin' told me you wasn't shooting skeets."

They checked the other buildings around the well and found the bodies of the two they'd killed.

Glory Boys. Each dead man with a red, white, and blue bandanna tied around his right arm. And government-issue automatic weapons. Government? If you could call it that. What was left of the government that had brought W.W. III down on the planet had holed up in a big underground shelter near what had once been Las Vegas. The Glory Boys were fanatically loyal to that ruthless government's remaining fragments, a few hundred military men and President Frayling, the ex-Hollywood-actor-turned-politician who'd hounded the Russians into a showdown fifteen years before. Frayling had escaped the burning of millions he'd brought down on the world. And most of the survivors hated him for that. They did business with the Glory Boys, his fighting elite and slave-taking outfit, but only reluctantly.

"So the Glory Boys are in on this," Link said. "Great. Just what we need. A bunch of fanatic redneck assholes."

"Look on the bright side," Traveler said as they pumped water into a bucket for the van. "Maybe they and the Road Wasps'll kill each other off."

"That'd be nice. Maybe Santa will bring us candy canes for Christmas."

And that's when they heard the roar of the engines.

6

Meet Me at the Cremation

Traveler and Link had just enough time to scavenge the dead Glory Boys' guns and ammo and back the van into the barn's deeper shadows before the Road Wasps roared into the corral.

The Spike rode in on her palanquin. Chained to the doorframe on her right was a nude Hispanic girl with long, glossy black hair, big, expressionless brown eyes, and a golden face marked with lines of stoic resignation. The Spike was wearing a pair of dusty goggles, which she pushed back on her grisly head as she got out of the palanquin-car—which reminded Traveler of a parade float—and went to the well. The bikers had parked protectively around her, and the souped-up wrecks driven by the seven other roadrats were parked in a rough circle around the bikes. The cars were piebald, patched together from the body parts of various models they'd found in scrap heaps. Frankenstein monsters among cars.

One of them was made from an old Dodge pickup truck. The truck's hood and fenders were missing, exposing the old V-6 engine, but the engine block and valve covers were painted yellow and black, in keeping with the Road Wasps' color motif. A yellow and black spike stuck out three feet from the radiator. There was a special harness chair up behind the driver's seat, where a gun sat up behind an oversized crossbow that poked up through a hole in the cab's roof. The gunner could launch three-foot hollow steel harpoons to a range of up to a hundred feet.

The gunner sat smoking smashweed and giggling, now and then reaching up to wipe dust off his goggles. He'd painted himself yellow, with black stripes around his eyes. The driver in front and below him got out and went to the back of the pickup. There was a cage in the rear, its metal bars toothed with spikes pointing in toward the prisoners. One of the prisoners wore a filthy sleeveless jacket and dreadlocks. His right eye was puffed, and he squatted on the floor looking miserable. "That's Jamaica Jack," Link said. "Musta got a map, come after the gold, and his rivals caught him." The other prisoners were two men Traveler thought he'd seen in The Fallout Shelter, the night the Old Man in the Hole had taken his vengeance with gold, and one road cannibal.

The roadrats busied themselves taking large quantities of the brackish water out of the well for their storage bladders, long bags of plastic in the trunks of their cars. Watching, stifling in the van, in the barn, in the heat of the afternoon, Traveler daydreamed about ice-cold Coors beer. Fifteen years since he'd had one.

"You think they'll check out the barn?" Link wondered.

"Probably they'll be in a hurry to get back on the trail of the gold."

They watched as the Spike strolled around to the other side of the palanquin car, leaned in under the fringed awning, and bit the nude Hispanic girl on her right breast. The girl closed her eyes and endured it. Clearly she took no pleasure in it.

"Christ," Link said. "What a shame. What a damn shame. . . ."

"Forget it," Traveler said firmly.

"Forget what?"

"What you were thinking."

"You reading minds now?"

"I could tell by the way you looked at that girl. Be practical. No way we're gonna rescue her and get that gold too. We can bend the odds, but you stack the odds too far against yourself and you're not even a bad gambler—you're just a corpse looking for a place to lie down."

Link said nothing.

The Spike straightened and patted the girl affectionately on the cheek and laughed. Then, carrying a sawed-off shotgun, she went to the prisoner's cage.

The Spike was wearing a kind of chain mail tunic and greasy rawhide pants with the buttocks cut out; there were tattoos of Japanese demons on her ass cheeks. In her nose was a heavy brass ring. Chains jangling, she went to the driver of the truck and bellowed an instruction. He was twice her height, but he scrambled to do her bidding, unlocking the rear of the cage.

Immediately, as the door swung outward, the road cannibal leaped from the cage and, shrieking gibberish, stark naked but for blue body paint, began to run.

He got twenty feet.

The Spike snarled and gave him one barrel from the sawed-off in the back. The cannibal wailed and fell on his face, his right lower back gouged raggedly open, spewing red. He lay writhing, clawing the dirt. The other roadrats hooted and laughed.

The Spike stalked up to him and shouted, "You made me waste a shotgun shell! Them things is hard to get!" She put her boot onto the wound in his back and began to grind her heel into it, pulping the little man's kidney. The cannibal screamed a long, trailing scream like the falling sound made by a bomb. He vomited into the dust and died. But she kept kicking.

In a few moments more, when his only movement was that of a dead meat kicked, she turned away and shouted, "Let 'em out!" at a man sitting in the back of a spike-covered convertible. *Literally* spike-covered—not two square inches showed without a spike. It made a sea urchin look like a baseball.

The other three prisoners were taken out of the truck and made to line up at its front end. They looked nervously at the corpse in the dust and then at the Spike and then at the buildings around them.

"Look like you're thinking about runnin'," the Spike bellowed. "I just might give you that chance."

As the driver stood guard—and the other roadrats watched, laughing, sitting in the shade of their vehicles and drinking a vile brew made which most human beings—something the roadrats had given up on years ago—would consider fermented garbage. The Spike climbed up into the cab of the truck and jerked the roadrat who was sitting at the harpoon launcher out of his seat, taking his place in the canvas harness. She cocked the harpoon gun and shouted, "Go ahead, run! This is your chance!"

Jamaica Jack ran for the barn.

The two prospectors looked at each other, hesitating— which was a mistake. The paunchy one on the right squealed and clutched at the harpoon shaft quivering in his belly, falling back with the impact, squirming in the dust like a pinned slug.

The Spike cackled, "Die like a man! Stop squealin', you wimp!" as she loaded another harpoon into the launcher. The two other prisoners were already running, in opposite directions; Jamaica Jack had a considerable lead, was nearly at the barn. She fired at him, and missed, the harpoon sailing past him to bury itself in the dirt beside the Meat Wagon. The other prospector, a short man with a gimpy leg, was limping as fast as he could toward the stable. She swung the harpoon around in a semicircle, reloaded, and launched it just before he reached the stable. The harpoon struck him in the back of the neck, passed through. He spun around, showing a foot of red-dripping steel protruding from the place where his Adam's apple had been, and then fell, twitching.

Jamaica Jack, in the meantime, had seen the Meat Wagon. "Traveler, shit! Help me and I give you my life, mon! I serve you! I do anything!" he shouted.

Traveler grated his teeth.

Link said, "Oh, fuck."

The Spike said, "Traveler? Did he say *Traveler*?"

Traveler started the van.

The roadrats got up and ran to their cars and bikes, reaching for their guns.

The Spike yelled hoarse orders.

Her driver got into the truck and started it, drove for the barn, was ten feet from the door when the Meat Wagon roared out into the corral.

The black van thudded a long machine gun burst at the throng of roadrats—Traveler timing the burst for the moment when he was precisely the right distance from them for the firing angle of his two guns to converge on his targets.

"Get down, baby," Link breathed as the machine guns strafed over the palanquin containing the nude female slave; the dark-eyed girl threw herself down in time, and the strafing line missed her.

But it didn't miss the two motorcycles roaring up behind it; bullet pocks appeared in the gas tank of the first, and it burst into flames, was a ball of flame on wheels heading for the barn. It crashed into the barn and set it afire. The second biker was smashed out of his seat, unhorsed by bullets.

The Spike had swung around, was coming hard on Traveler's tail. She launched a harpoon at his right rear tire, but the spear stuck in the chain mail skirts over the wheels and dragged behind the van, leaving a snake track in the dirt as Traveler veered in and out of clusters of the enemy, and then swung hard left, around the well, and down the dirt road between the stable and the desert.

But the road didn't go out into the desert from here. He had to get through town first to get to the road leading out of the valley. The Road Wasps were hard on his heels, and bullets whined off the armoring at the rear of the van, narrowly missing Jamaica Jack, who was clinging to the back door.

They split up, some of them cutting through alleys between buildings to roar at him from the sides. The spike-covered car had cut through and come out ahead of him, as he swung into town along what had been Main Street. The roadrat riding shotgun in the spiked car pulled a lever, and steel gouging arms swung out from slots in the side. They were L-shaped, the short segment of the *L* sharpened and pointing forward.

Traveler swerved, dodging the four-foot reach of the gouger; but it dug into the left side of the van as it swept past, plowing a one-inch-deep scratch the length of the Meat Wagon.

Traveler cursed. "Completely fucked up my paint job now! You'll pay for that you mother cocksucker!" And he pulled off a U-turn so abrupt the van felt like it was going up on two wheels, Link was thrown against the door, and Jamaica Jack was wrenched from his hold, and spun whimpering into the dirt.

Traveler drove hard at the rear of the spiked-over car ahead.

"What you doing, man!" Link shouted.

"You see what kind of car that is under the spikes?" Traveler asked. "That's a—"

He rammed the Meat Wagon into the rear of the smaller vehicle, the ramming wedge crunching into the back—and the car exploded into a ball of fire.

"—an old Ford Pinto!" Traveler finished, backing away from the conflagration.

He fired a burst from the overhead guns at the Spike as her pickup drove at him. She veered to avoid the strafing, and he gunned by her.

And then they were surrounded.

It was usually a mistake to lose your temper in a road

fight. He'd lost his temper with the Pinto and had come around to chase it, and now they were surrounded, the roadrats driving in circles around them as they pulled up at the end of the street.

The air was tortured with engine roarings and gunshots and the squeals of tires and protesting brakes and the whine of ricocheting bullets. A cloud of dust distorted the scene into a hellish whirl of angular metal, muzzle flashes, snarling faces, and billowing yellow. Link fired through the hole in the windshield, knocking another biker off his three-wheeler, which plowed driverless through the rotten wall of what had once been a general store. The building collapsed over it, as if throwing up its hands in despair. The Pinto had crashed into a saloon, and the fire, leaping hungrily to the old building, was minutes later spreading to the others, eagerly cremating the dead town.

And all the while the ring of lethal metal was tightening around Traveler and Link.

"No way we gonna make it!" Link shouted.

Traveler glimpsed Jamaica Jack, forgotten by the roadrats, sprinting into a crumbling bank building at the other end of the street.

And Traveler saw something else, something that held his attention: an enemy coming to his rescue.

The dragster was roaring down the street, on the left side, someone inside firing an assault rifle in skillful bursts at the roadrats, picking off the last biker and the driver of the pickup. The pickup veered out of control and piled into a graying wall. The building collapsed around it. But moments later, the Spike emerged, dusting herself off and cursing Traveler, who was roaring through the gap made by the dragster and down the main street to the road out of town. The dragster fired another burst into the roadrats and swung around to follow.

Traveler slowed to take the curve—and then squealed to a stop when Jamaica Jack ran out in front of him, waving his arms.

"All right, all right, get in!" Traveler growled.

Link opened the side door and let the frantic little man crawl over him to the back. Then they burnt rubber, burning out of town and into the desert leaving blood, fire, and dust behind.

Rushing forward straight into the loving arms of the Glory Boys.

7

You're in the Army Now

They were ringed in by an army of government-issue hoodlums.

Up ahead, a jeep blocked the way. Two men stood behind a fifty-caliber heavy machine gun mounted on the rear of the jeep.

Traveler and the dragster pulled up short, looking around.

To both sides the road was lined with Glory Boys, maybe a hundred of them, a gauntlet, armed and ready, guns in hands, waiting for the order to commence firing. The three trucks they'd arrived in were parked behind them.

"You get the feeling the Army is seriously going after that gold?" Link asked.

"Yah, yah, the Glory Boys took a gold-plate map from Slasher. Beat the shit out of him for it," Jamaica Jack said, from behind.

Traveler turned to look at him. "You want to surrender to the Glory Boys?"

"And end up in some underground lab as a guinea pig, mon? No thanks."

"Then take that Remington there. Pump-action 12-gauge riot shotgun. You know how to use it?"

Jack nodded and picked up the shotgun. A bullhorn voice thundered from the jeep, *"Get out of the vehicles with your hands up. You will not be hurt. This is the United States Army."*

"Lying motherfuckers," Traveler said, under his breath. It pissed him off when they pretended to be legitimate Army.

"Get out of the vehicles . . ."

Traveler glanced at the dragster, wondering what it would do.

The silvery, dust-streaked vehicle, low to the ground and steaming with the heat of its idling engine, had pulled up close to his left. There were two passengers, both wearing goggles, scarves over their mouths. The driver wore black leather driving gloves; the other man wore a torn *Clash* T-shirt, from the eighties. There was a tattoo on his right arm that somehow looked familiar. . . .

Traveler peered at them through the firing slit and said, just loud enough for them to hear, "You giving up?"

Both dragster passengers simply shook their heads.

"We'll give you one more chance to surrender!" the voice boomed from the bullhorn.

Traveler shouted out the window at the jeep, *"We want to pull up closer to parley! Don't shoot!"*

"There will be no parley. Unconditional surrender—"

"Don't shoot! We want to discuss terms!" Traveler shouted, hoping that would slow them down for a minute.

Moving very slowly, crawling along, the Meat Wagon and the dragster inched closer to the jeep. As they went, they moved gradually apart, so each vehicle had a passing route open on either side of the jeep. A man in a green helmet and blue-tinted goggles stood on the running board of the jeep, megaphone in hand, thundering, *"Come no closer! This is your last warning!"*

Traveler paused, just ten feet from the jeep. The dragster pulled up too. "We're going to throw our weapons out!" he shouted.

He whispered to Link, "Hand me those SMGs we took off their outriders."

"Sad waste of goods, my man," Link said, passing over two submachine guns. But he held the AR15 across his lap, out of sight below the dashboard. Traveler slid back the vertical steel firing slit on the door and pushed the guns through, one at a time, adding a pistol he'd taken from a Road Wasp. The guns clattered to the ground.

The captain in the jeep turned to the dragster. "Okay— you two—toss yours out too!"

As the bullhorn roared, Traveler slid the Colt off his hip and propped it in the firing slit. The machine gunners in the back of the jeep were looking at the dragster.

But one of the Glory Boys beside the road shouted, "Hey this one's still got a gun!" Raising an M16, pointing it at Traveler . . .

Traveler and Link fired at the same moment, Traveler squeezing off three shots at the three men in the jeep, Link firing a burst at the man to their right with the M16. The three in the jeep went down without

73

firing a shot, each man with a neat red hole through his forehead.

Because, yeah, Traveler was that good.

And the "Army" thug with the M16 spun around, yelling, as Link's burst cut him in half.

Traveler gunned the van ahead as the dragster cut loose with its assault weapon, blasting out the jeep's tires and three Glory Boys who'd run up to fire after the van. And then it was roaring past Traveler on the dirt road, waving as if to say, "So long, sucker!" And Traveler wondered if that contemptuous wave was meant for him or the Glory Boys. Or both.

Jamaica Jack fired two rounds at the Glory Boys running after them, shooting out the firing slit in the rear door.

"Yo, thas two Glory Boys less," he cackled.

"What happened to the Road Wasps?" Link asked, as the Meat Wagon picked up speed.

"They saw the Glory Boys, they probably took a powder," Traveler said. "But they'll be on our tail, too. We'll have them, the so-called Army, and a lot of other scumbags to play with on the way."

"I guess we won't have to sing, 'One hundred Bottles of Beer on the Wall,'" Link said cheerily.

Traveler gave him a disgusted look.

Jamaica Jack came up toward the front, leaned over the back seats, crowing, "Them Army bastards, they're nothing, eh? We made them fools!"

"They're not Army," Traveler said. "If they were, we'd never have got out of there in one piece, without surrendering. . . . Now sit down in back and shut up. I don't need you breathing dope fumes down my neck. First opportunity, we let you off."

74

"But, mate, they'll kill me—!"

"So we'll let you off at night, give you some food and water, you sneak across country back to Drift."

"I can be real valuable, Traveler—"

"Only if we need to jettison ballast."

"Traveler," Link said, "What do you think made those dragster dudes help us out?"

Traveler shook his head. "I can't figure it. Maybe a whim. Maybe they just hate roadrats. Looks like the partnership is off, anyway—they're gone."

The dragster had outstripped them, racing ahead to dwindle into a tiny cloud of dust, and then nothing at all. It was lost over the horizon.

It was a big horizon, here. They'd passed out of the valley, over the ridge, and entered Cattle Ivory Flats. It was a salt flat, cracked in crisscrossing patterns, barren as the soul of a banker, its yellow-white distances shimmying in heat waves rising from the baking earth. The road ran straight ahead. There wasn't much cover, in this country: the occasional patch of scrub or clump of boulders; here and there a shallow gulley, or a rusted car-hulk. Even these scant features were few and far between.

"Van breaks down here," Link said, "We're dead meat."

"Yeah," Traveler agreed. "But there's no turning back. The Glory Boys'll take a while to get their lunkheads into those trucks, but they'll be right along. I figure maybe thirty minutes behind . . ."

They were another hour on the road, the sun beginning to flirt with the blue hills at the horizon, when they saw the wreck up ahead.

A thin column of smoke rose from an overturned

station wagon. There were bodies scattered around it, sprawled out in the sun, bloating.

Traveler could see the track marks where the dragster had cut around the wreck and continued on, up the road. From the look of the track, the dragster hadn't even paused.

"A good policy," Traveler said softly, whipping the Meat Wagon off the road to follow suit.

They circled through the desert, around the wreckage, then back onto the road. Link got in the back to look at the wreckage through the rear firing slit.

"There's somebody alive back there," he said. "Looks like a woman. Hurt. Waving at us."

Traveler said, "So fucking *what*?"

"So—we've got to be more than the rest of these people, Traveler. You know what I mean, man? We can't just . . .just leave her out there to die. . . ."

"You want the gold or not? You want something, you have to set your sights on it and follow through. And that means ignoring all distractions."

"Yeah," said Jamaica Jack, "Traveler is right. It's foolish, you know, to go back there."

Traveler hit the brake. The van squealed to a halt. "On the other hand, Link," he said. "If the quasi-Rastafarian says I should go on, maybe I should go back."

"You were just looking for an excuse," Link said, as Traveler U-turned the van and drove back to the wreckage. He pulled up a cautious thirty feet off and surveyed the scene.

It was a big Chrysler station wagon, once two-tone yellow and gold flake, now spotted with rust and scorch marks and crumpled-in places. It was lying on its right side; the underside, grimy and blackened, faced Traveler.

There was a woman lying in the shade of the over-turned car, face down, her hair spilled around her head like milk: her hair was milk-white. She raised a hand feebly to them, and then let it drop.

Traveler frowned. There'd been something just a touch dramatic about the motion.

Link got out, carrying the M16. Traveler opted for his crossbow. He'd scavenged it from an old sporting goods store. It was about the size of a sawed-off shotgun; the one-piece stock was made of glass-filled polypropy-lene; the stock was outfitted with a thumbhole pistol grip. The steel prod fired 8-inch arrows.

He fitted an arrow into the bow and stuck four others in his belt.

Link was bending over the woman with the white hair.

Traveler got out of the van. He spoke through the open door to Jamaica Jack. "Stay inside. Watch the van. But don't fuck with anything, there are booby traps." And he took the ignition key with him.

Traveler walked toward the overturned car, thinking: Those bodies on the other side of the car have been dead at least a day. . . .

Traveler looked at the desert to either side of the road. He saw nothing.

But that didn't mean that nothing was there.

Traveler cocked the crossbow and approached Link and the fallen woman. "What's the story with her?"

"I dunno," Link said. "She seems dazed."

The woman was strangely pale, her eyes milky-blue. She wore an ancient pair of overalls. Her hands and feet were grimy with dirt. The dirt, Traveler noted, didn't look like the yellow dust of the flats.

"Can you walk, Lady?" Traveler asked, coming to stand beside Link.

She made a long, strange cawing sound then, turning her face toward the left side of the road.

"It's a set-up, Link!" Traveler hissed, spinning to the left.

The desert was opening up.

Yard-square sections of the desert tilted back. Sand and dirt spilled away from camouflaged wooden trap doors. Three doors, six feet apart, opened in the sands, and white-haired men poured from them, holding weighted hand-held nets like gladiator's snares. The pallid, rag-clothed men carried the nets with a special knob woven into the mesh. The outside of the nets were sticky with some kind of homemade glue. They whipped them expertly overhead, flung them, and two of the snares enwrapped Link like living things, tangling his arms.

Traveler sidestepped a net, which fell on the white-haired woman; she whined as she struggled to escape it.

The twelve men kept coming. They were white-haired but not old, and they had more than nets. They carried bladed boomerangs, razor-sharp, which they snapped at Traveler's legs. He leaped up, and two silvery whirling slashers flashed beneath him and sank into the dirt behind him. He recovered, leaped to the left, evading another boomerang, and fired the crossbow at the nearest man. It caught him in the mouth and he fell, blood dripping along the shaft quivering between his teeth. Traveler stopped the next ambusher with a solid kick to

78

the jaw. The man stumbled back, carrying down two of his friends, giving Traveler time to fit another shaft into the crossbow and fire. And again, and again, firing his remaining arrows in three seconds, one after the other, to deadly effect. Three men went down, arrows quivering in their chests.

But there were at least half a dozen more closing in on him.

"Jack!" Traveler shouted. "Get the fuck out here!"

Two nets whipped down at him from overhead. He managed to elude one of them, but the other came straight for his head—he had time only to punch his left arm out into it, tangling the arm and making the fingers of his left hand useless, but keeping the mesh away from the rest of him. He slammed the crossbow into the temple of his nearest assailant, gaining time to get to Link, who was kicking at two of the men trying to pull him down.

They want us alive, Traveler realized. They could have killed Link with their blades. And they'd thrown the boomerangs at Traveler's legs, not his vitals.

There was a short, pale, white-haired man clinging to Link's back, trying to drag him down, and another slugging him in the belly.

Traveler plucked his shuriken throwing stars from his belt with his free hand and flung them, one-two, at the two men on Link. The first sank in the neck of the man clinging to Link's back. The man hissed with pain and fell away, clawing at his spurting neck; the second throwing star sank into the other man's right eye. He howled and staggered away, his face in his hands.

Link's M16 was tangled under the net, pointing

upwards. Traveler evaded another flung net, dodged a boomerang, and shouted, "Bend at the waist, Link!"

Link bent, Traveler stepped behind him and reached through the mesh to fire the M16 at the remaining attackers, blasting between the skeins, raking back and forth. Two men went down, shot to pieces. A third went to his knees, wounded. The fourth leaped down a hatch into the blind.

Jamaica Jack ran up, carrying the shotgun. "You need me?"

Traveler looked at him in annoyance. "Fast action."

"Hey, mon, you say stay in the van—"

"Just—finish off those two, the ones with the throwing stars, and any others you find here still alive. . . . That one over there's just out cold. So is that one. . . . Naw, don't kill those two. Just the badly wounded ones. Use a knife."

"I got to do that?"

"Make yourself useful or start walking."

Jamaica Jack sighed and drew his knife. Traveler took the shotgun and turned away.

He gathered his shuriken and went to the man kneeling at the side of the road. One of the M16 rounds had torn a hunk out of his left thigh. "Looks like it missed the artery," Traveler said. "You'll live, if you don't get gangrene. And if I don't let you bleed to death."

The man was dressed in grimy overalls, his shoulders bare. On his forehead was a blue, badly made tattoo. Probably done with a needle and ink. It showed the outline of a digging spade. The man was gaunt, white-haired, but not older than forty. He had a small forked beard of dried-out white hair and milky blue eyes. At first he glared defiantly at Traveler—but when he heard the other wounded men shrieking as Jamaica Jack sloppily put them to death, he lowered his eyes.

No need to unnecessarily aggravate the victor.

Traveler pointed the shotgun at him. "You want to live?"

Grudgingly, the gaunt man nodded his head.

"Then explain some things. What's that tattoo on your head mean? The others don't have it."

"I am the chief of the digmen."

"You people are digmen?"

The man nodded miserably. "Please . . . ." He swayed. "I feel very . . . sick."

"Yeah, a bullet in the leg'll do that to you. . . . How do we get this fucking net off?"

"If you have kerosene, or gasoline, that dissolves the glue."

"Jack!" Traveler shouted. "Bring me a can of kerosene!"

"But—the booby traps!" Jack pointed out.

"You have a point. Take Link with you. He can tell you how to take the thing out. . . ." Traveler turned to the digman chief. "How many others down there?"

"Three ferrets, five mates, two cubs."

"Ferrets? Oh, your warriors. Go ahead and call for help. They won't be hurt unless they try to fuck with us again."

The chief shouted, "Kracko! Breeder! We have a truce! Come! Bring bandages!"

"And make it unarmed!" Traveler shouted.

Reluctantly, blinking in the sunlight, two men came out of the burrows carrying strips of cloth and an herbal paste. They carried their chief to the shade of the overturned station wagon and ministered to him.

Jamaica Jack returned with Link and the kerosene.

Link swore as they doused him, adding, "No smoking, you guys, all right?" Three minutes later the nets were cleared away, and Link and Traveler were toweling off.

"Glory Boys'll be here soon," Link said.

"I'm surprised they're not here already," Traveler admitted. "Probably got hung up arguing about who was in charge after we offed their captain. They're terminally disorganized."

Traveler turned to the wounded chieftain. "Tell your people to come up here. All of them. I'm gonna look over their burrow."

The chief scowled but did as he was told. Five women and two little girls came up, blinking, shivering with fear.

Link turned to the leader. "Why'd you want us alive? Slavery?"

The chief shook his head. "So you could mate with our women. We need breeding blood from outside."

Link grinned. "Then why all the elaborate trap-setting? Why didn't you just open a bordello or put up a sign? Lot of fellow's be happy to accommodate you."

"The Earthgod requires that we sacrifice the new breeder by bleeding him to death and feeding the blood to the thirsty earth, after he has done the deed. You would not have minded?"

"Ah . . . when you put it that way, actually, I think I'd have passed on it. . . ."

Traveler said, "Jack, you watch over the tribe here, and try not to get sacrificed to the Earthgod. Anybody moves quick, cut 'em down." He passed the little man the shotgun. "Come on, Link, let's check out the Earthgod's digs."

*　　*　　*

The frames of wrecked cars had been used as the support beams for the underground passageways. Animal-fat candles lit the way with soft yellow light from wall niches. The floor underfoot was packed earth. It was cool here, relief from the heat up above. They followed the passage about twenty feet back till it opened into a foul-smelling chamber about thirty feet by forty. Beds of rags and car seats were laid out along both walls. The stores were sparse; a few tin cans, a pot of rotting meat. "I get the feeling they haven't been here long, maybe don't plan to stay long," Traveler remarked.

"They wouldn't find much traffic to prey on out in this godforsaken desert," Link said. "You know what I think? I think the Old Man In the Hole cued them that a lot of people would be coming this way. One of his little surprises."

"Yeah, you're probably right—Hey look at this!"

He'd found an old crate, four feet by two, in the back of a sort of closet dug into the wall. Pulling it out, they opened it, and looked at each other, grinning.

It was filled with dynamite, and fuses.

The chief wasn't pleased to see Traveler and Link carrying the crate of dynamite up the ladder and out into the open. "That is very important to us," he said. "A great treasure. Please, you must not take it!"

"You want favors from people, you should stop trying to bleed them for the Earthgod," Link said, as they began to pack the dynamite into the station wagon.

"What are you doing?" The chief asked, sitting up, alarmed.

"Take your people back underground," Traveler said. "In a little while, you'll hear explosions. Have a cautious look around, you'll probably find some prospects for breeding and bleeding. But don't come up till you hear the blasts."

The digmen, under Jamaica Jack's watchful eye, went grumbling but obediently back underground. At Traveler's instructions, Jamaica Jack covered the trapdoors with sand and dirt, concealing them once more.

"Maybe we shouldn't have let them take that girl, the one in the net," Jamaica Jack said. "We could make them bring her back up again. She could be Big Fun, brother-man."

"Just get in the van and wait," Traveler said. "We've got enough dead weight along already."

Jamaica Jack frowned and turned away. There was anger in his walk as he went back to the van.

Link watched him go. "Not smart to put a man down when you got to have him at your back, Traveler," he said, as he packed dynamite under the hood of the station wagon.

"I've got no patience with diplomacy anytime," Traveler said. "Less now than ever before. This whole thing has been a royal pain in the ass. One fucking thing after another. And some intuition, some little hunch, some sneaky insight, tells me it's going to get worse before it gets better."

The truth was, Traveler's NT77-frayed nerves were acting up. The pressure of human company was getting to him.

Ought to stop kidding myself, he thought. I'm a loner. I don't need Link, or anyone else. Anyplace I go, the killing starts. Ought to do everyone a favor and stay the hell away from people except when I need food and gas. . . .

84

But he couldn't help thinking of Jan. Lithe, doe-eyed Jan. Jan with her strong, smooth limbs. Her small, perfect ass, her razor-sharp reflexes, her cool confidence, her soft lips, her quick mind.

Traveler sighed. It had been too long . . .

"Maybe I just need to get laid," he said, as he dug the trench from the car to the kerosene can, on the south side of the wreck.

"Well, don't look at *me*, man," Link said, as he went to inspect the bodies of the dead men lying on the north side of the station wagon. They'd been bled dry, all right, and the shape of a down-pointed cross whose lower end opened into a digging shovel had been carved into each man's chest.

"Guess we'll never know who they were," Link said, turning away. He stared down the road. "Shit, Traveler. . . . Here they come."

Traveler was relighting the fire the digmen had set in the wagon; it had been part of the lure to make the wreck look like a fresh one. It might work again.

The two men hurried back to the van and got in. Forty feet down the road a large boulder abutted the roadside. Just big enough to hide the Meat Wagon.

Traveler backed the van up behind the boulder and got out, carrying the M16.

He went to stand by the boulder, hidden by its granite outthrust, peering through a crack at the station wagon.

Three green Army trucks were just pulling up to check out the wreck. Ignoring the shouts of one of their officers, the Glory Boys piled out, hooting, hoping to find fresh slaves or loot in the station wagon.

Scavenging and salvaging were more than customary

in the post-W.W. III world. They were necessities of life. Everyone did it, at any opportunity. Which is what Traveler was counting on.

The men moved in close around the car; forty, fifty of them, poking at it . . .

Two of them stood staring at the trench Traveler had filled with kerosene and then at the can the trench led to. They turned their heads to follow the line of the shallow trench back to the station wagon, to the bundle of fuses . . .

And then they ran, shouting a warning.

At the same moment, Traveler sighted in on the gas can and fired. The first shot failed to blow the can, merely punching a hole in it. Traveler cursed and tried again. The second round struck a spark, and the gas can went up in a pillar of fire. The golden-red flame leaped onto the kerosene trench; the blue-tipped flame ran along the trench to the short fuses, soaked with kerosene. Men ran, but not fast enough.

Traveler ducked back behind the boulder as the crate of TNT blew, a flame-thorny fireball engulfing the car and most of the men around it, the shock wave blowing a dozen others into the air and into pieces, and over-turning one of the trucks, setting another afire. Traveler stepped out onto the road and expended his clip picking off running, confused Glory Boys and blowing out the tires of the remaining vehicle.

Then he ran to the passenger-side door of the van, as Link brought it out onto the road, and they raced away, due Southwest, into the thickening twilight, under the sad lamp of sunset.

*　　　*　　　*

They were driving through darkness, looking for a place to camp. Traveler didn't want to risk another ambush, something that was all too likely in the dark.

Jamaica Jack spoke for the first time in two hours.

"There's something maybe you oughta know, Brother-man," he said.

"What's that?" Traveler asked, reaching for patience. Why didn't the guy just say it outright?

"Those digmen people, I hear them talking. They migrate, from one dig-hole to another. And there are many tribes of them. Fallout shelter people, with a crazy leader. Had him visions of a devil-Jah. And they say there are more in the hills, waiting."

"That's just great," Traveler said.

And that's when he saw the campfires.

8

Queen Wasp's Dream Come True

"What do you think?" Link said. "Should we take a look?"

Traveler shrugged. "There's a gully over there, if I make it out right. We can camp there. With luck, those campfires'll cover for us. Anybody comes along, they'll see them, not us. We'll keep lights out. The campfires'll take the hassle if anyone nasty's about."

"We're gonna need gas soon," Link pointed out. "We got only two cans left and what's in the tank, which isn't much. We might swipe it from that camp."

"First things first." Traveler switched off his head-light and turned right, driving cautiously toward the gully. There was a little starlight picking out the high-lights of the flats. The gully ran at right angles to the road. Just south of it was a slight swell in the land, not more than fifteen feet above the surrounding flats. On the other side of the swell someone had laid out three campfires, probably thinking the landswell would hide them from the road. But Traveler had seen the telltale flicker of sparks rising, and the faint glow along the crest.

"What the hell are they using for wood?" Link wondered.

"Roadrats carry fuel for campfires," Traveler said. "They live in the open most of the time."

He drove with painful slowness, peering ahead for obstructions, and not wanting to make much engine noise.

The van rumbled softly as they rolled into the shallow gully, an erosion runoff cut around the north edge of the landswell. It was barely deep enough to hide the Meat Wagon.

Traveler pulled up in the deepest place along the gully's fifty-yard length.

The heat of the day was a distant memory. It was chill, now, and inky dark here. As their eyes adjusted, they made camp, using a muted kerosene lantern for light as they opened tin cans—beans canned fifteen years before—and shared them. Traveler made sure that Jamaica Jack got an equal share. But still the little mulatto said nothing.

They sat with their backs to the Meat Wagon, wishing there were still such things as cigarette manufacturers. All three men were wrapped in a deep, bone-aching fatigue. How many fights had there been that day? Traveler was too weary to be sure. . . .

He woke at the urging of his internal timer. It was maybe an hour before dawn; the sky at the east showed the faintest suggestion of aluminum gray.

He'd fallen asleep sitting up against the van. His back

ached. He stood, stretching cramps out of it. He yearned for coffee.

But there were other ways to get your adrenaline flowing.

He picked up his crossbow and arrows and checked the load on the .45 in his hip holster. He'd forgotten that once and had almost died. He had decided then that that one mistake was all he'd allow himself.

He glanced at Link. He was still asleep in his sleeping bag. Jamaica Jack had no bedroll. He'd asked Traveler if he could sleep in the van. Traveler thought about checking on him and shrugged it off.

The campfires had burnt down to winking coals and a little smoke rising thinly to add its darkness to the sky's. Men were stretched out snoring around the heaps of golden embers. Other slept in the cars, parked on the flatter ground a short distance west. Traveler saw only one sentry, pacing near a pickup. The pickup . . .

He frowned. There was a cage in the back of the pickup. So they'd pulled it out from under the wrecked building. And this was the Road Wasps' camp. They must have come cross-country, Traveler realized. They'd passed the Meat Wagon well off the road while he was dealing with the digmen. There were only five or six men and the queen left. And maybe that Chicano slave.

So now what?

Kill them. He had the advantage of surprise. He had several weapons on him. He could kill most of them before they were fully awake. And then he'd have their fuel, their food, and most important he'd have eliminated them before they could eliminate him.

Traveler was crouched in an erosion rut at the northern head of the gully, looking up at the roadrats camp. To his right, forty feet away, was the cluster of parked cars. He didn't see a motorcycle.

The sentry stood beside the palanquin-car, a shotgun cradled in his arms. Now and then he strolled a few feet on, looked around, shuffled back.

First the sentry.

Traveler waited till the man decided to move on, looking over the campsite, his back to Traveler. The sentry put a hand to his mouth to stifle a yawn.

Traveler moved like flowing oil over the terrain, soundless, his motions smooth, keeping low.

The trick was to silence the man the same time as you killed him. And that meant precision crossbow shooting. He must be killed instantaneously, so that no dying-man's reflex set off the shotgun, warning the others.

And that meant severing the medulla, where the spinal cord met the brain. Cut the puppet's strings.

Traveler moved in closer still, twelve feet away now. He could hear the man humming faintly under his breath. Could hear him breathe. Surely the sentry must hear him coming.

But you didn't allow yourself to think about that. If you lost your nerve, your muscles stiffened, contracting with tension; if that happened, your movements were clumsy, you sent a message to the sentry by dislodging a pebble or crunching your boot in the sand at the crucial moment.

The ideal killer is calm, deliberate, concentrated, totally focused on his objective. And the men who'd fought with Kiel Paxton, whom men now called Traveler, in a dozen secret CIA-sponsored Special Forces engagements nearly two decades before—any one of those men would have testified that the perfect killer was a guy named Paxton.

Traveler was crouched six feet from the sentry. He stood, slowly, aimed the crossbow at the back of the man's neck.

"There he is! Like I said, Spike!" came the piping voice from behind.

The sentry whirled. Traveler fired. The crossbow bolt sped home, splitting the sentry's Adam's apple so he fell choking, strangling on his own blood.

Traveler reached for his Colt, at the same time spinning about to see who'd spoken.

Jamaica Jack was there, and with him was the Spike, queen of the Road Wasps.

In the face of treachery even the perfect killer is helpless.

Traveler snarled and raised the Colt. But two men leaped at him from the sides, smashing him with clubs, and he went down in a kaleioscopic whirl of blazing spots and blazing pain.

He lay on his back, stunned but conscious, trying to sort out the flashes caused by the clubs from the gleam of stars overhead.

The field of stars was eclipsed by the brutal face of the Spike, who stood over him, looking down at him, grinning horribly, her eyes shining with bestial interior light.

"You should've checked those blankets by the camp-fire," she said mockingly. "Half of 'em are empty! And you're supposed to be such a pro! If this moron hadn't yapped at the last moment, we wouldn't have lost that sentry. But he'll pay, and you will too. . . . My my, but it's good to see you, Traveler! I've been daydreaming about what I'd do to you if I had you in my hands! Now my dream's going to come true!"

"If you plan to rape me," Traveler said raspily, "do me a favor and kill me first."

She kicked him in the head for that, and he lost both the flashes and the gleams.

9

The Roadrats Invite
Traveler to a Party

When Traveler woke, his first thought was that they must have broken his brain because things were upside down. And then he saw that it was only that what he was looking at was upside down—Jamaica Jack. The mulatto was hanging by his ankles from a wooden stake. His arms were lashed to the stake below his head. His dreadlocks hung down to mingle with the dirt. He was nude, and whimpering.

It was dawn. Traveler's head pulsed with a pain brighter than the rising desert sun.

He was lying on his back, staked down with four sticks and rawhide thongs. Spread-eagled. He looked around, expecting to see Link in the same predicament. "Link!" Traveler called weakly.

"I'm here, man, behind you. We're tied head to head. . . . We're together like that because we're both so fucking stupid."

Traveler tested his bonds. The stakes were buried

deeply in the hard-packed earth; he was spread-eagled at an awkward angle, a position that made it impossible for him to get the leverage he'd need to break loose. So he stopped trying, conserving his strength, waiting for an opportunity.

Thinking about that, he almost laughed out loud at himself. An opportunity? Staked down and unarmed in the middle of the desert with no one around but half a dozen kill-crazy, drugged-out maniacs thirsting for his blood and watching him every second?

"You know what, Link?" he said, as he absently watched the roadrats prepare hot irons in the campfires, "I think this is serious."

Link laughed. And Traveler remembered why he liked the man.

"They lied to me!" Jamaica Jack wailed. "Said they'd make me a Road Wasp. They will be punished! . . . It is the judgment of Jah!"

"If there's a Jah," Link growled, "he's gonna kick your ass right out the door when you get to Rasta paradise, Jack."

Jack didn't reply. He was distracted.

Hot irons are distracting.

He screamed as the Spike pressed the white-hot metal to his crotch. She let it sizzle there for a while, then returned it to the fire, picked up another in her gloved hand, and held it up so Traveler could see it glowing white against the deep blue sky.

"You see that, Traveler? Watch what we do to him, and think about what it's going to be like when it's your turn!"

"Take your time with him," Traveler said. "I wouldn't want to miss anything."

96

"You'll lose that smirk when you start screaming," the Spike said, as she turned to apply the hot iron once more to Jamaica Jack.

The four roadrats around the Spike chugged some foul brew and smoked smashweed and staggered about, from time to time kicking Jamaica Jack in the head or pissing in his open wounds.

A sentry stood beside Traveler. He wandered off to get himself a drink from the truck.

And then something strange: Traveler heard Link talking in Spanish, very softly.

And he heard a feminine voice replying in a whisper.

Traveler lifted his head a little and managed to look over his right shoulder enough to see that the palanquin-car was parked near Link. The Chicano slavegirl was sitting in the seat, chained to the doorframe, talking to Link. Then a faint metallic sound as something was dropped from the car near Link's arm.

"Shit," Link muttered.

"What's up?" Traveler asked, as if he were passing the time of day.

"She dropped me a knife, from the car. But I can't quite reach it, and she can't reach down to help, her chain's too short."

"How close is it to your fingers?"

"Three inches out of reach."

Traveler's wrists were bound to the stake, but his fingers were free. Trying to get loose, he'd touched something in the sand. . . . He probed for it again. There it was. A stick. Just a twig, five inches long.

He picked it up awkwardly between two fingers and flipped it backwards, aiming for Link's hands.

The stick fell on Link's wrist. After some wriggling,

he got hold of it and used it to pull the short-bladed knife near. He got the knife between two fingers and began sawing. The sentry had paused at the stake to take a turn with Jamaica Jack. He used a can opener to saw open the little man's abdomen, letting the glistening intestines flop out, blood-spattered. Jamaica Jack gave a final squeal and lost consciousness.

"Hurry it up, Link," Traveler whispered urgently. "They're losing interest in their little game. The game just conked out."

"Doing the best I can. Tough to cut from this angle."

They were slapping the mulatto now, trying to wake him.

"Shit goddamnit," the Spike snarled. "The little wimp died on me! Well, take him down and we'll put Traveler up there and we'll take more time with him! We'll do Traveler *real carefully!*"

The roadrats hooted with delight at that.

Traveler heard a twanging sound as a rawhide cord parted.

And then a scuffing noise as Link twisted about to cut his other bonds.

The bitch is going to turn around and see Link getting loose and bring her scum down on him before he makes it, Traveler thought.

The Spike was lighting a thumb-sized smashweed joint. She inhaled deeply, blinked, and her squat face seemed to get uglier, slacker. She stalked over to Traveler and bent to blow smoke in his face. Then she noticed Link had changed positions. The dope slowed her reactions, and it was a full two seconds before she shouted.

"This one's getting loose!"

By that time Link had cut the ropes on his ankles.

The roadrats had turned, gaping, were gathering themselves together to charge. Cocking rifles, raising crossbows. Unarmed, Link didn't have a chance. So he did the only sensible thing.

He ran.

He sprinted off into the desert and in seconds was gone from sight over the top of the rise.

"You see that, Traveler!" the queen Wasp bellowed. "Your loyal pal ran off and deserted you! Seem like all your pals betray you, you arrogant son of a bitch!"

The roadrats had staggered off to chase Link—but the queen Wasp called them back. "Forget that black chickenshit! We'll track him later! He can't get far! We got the key to the van! He can't drive it! He'll set off on foot, and we'll track his black ass down! Let's deal with the Big Brave Hero here first!"

Reprieved from an irksome task, the roadrats came cackling back and cut Traveler loose. Then—one of them pressing a shotgun to his forehead—they carried him to the stake and began to strip him in preparation for tying him onto it.

And that's when Traveler heard a familiar sound. The roar of the Meat Wagon's engine turning over, echoing to them from the gully.

Link knew how to get past Traveler's booby traps and how to hot-wire a car.

So Link would get away, at least. Traveler shrugged and decided to force the issue here. Let them shoot him. It was better than dying by torture.

He smashed an elbow into the gut of the man holding him from behind. The man buckled, gagging. The Spike

99

shouted, "Don't shoot him, hold him! I want him on the stake! Hold him so I can—"

The words froze on her lips. She was staring at something over Traveler's shoulder. Something behind him.

Then Traveler heard the roar of the Meat Wagon, as it barreled hard at them, and the sound of a blasting Stooges tape in the player. The wasps had taken the ammo from the overhead guns, but they'd left the sonic ammunition. The roadrats were paralyzed with confusion, just long enough.

Traveler wrenched free and threw himself aside. The Meat Wagon roared through the camp and plowed into the cluster of roadrats beside the stake.

They mingled their screams as its bumper-spikes ripped into them, its ramming wedge smashed them, its wheels crushed them.

Traveler got to his feet in time to see the Spike and a tall, brawny roadrat with a red beard running for the nearest vehicle downhill from them. The pickup.

Traveler looked around and saw the weapons they'd taken from the Meat Wagon stacked in the palanquin-car. He found the M16, still loaded and ran with it after the pickup.

The two roadrats were just scrambling into the truck.

Traveler raised the gun, sighted in, and—click. The bastard had hung fire again. Traveler took the rifle by the barrel and smashed it on a boulder, splintering the stock and cracking the breach.

"Shit, man, take the clip out before you do that!" Link said reproachfully.

Traveler tossed the broken weapon aside in disgust. "That was stupid. We could have sold it. And the bitch got away."

"Grab a couple guns and climb in, we'll go after 'em."

Traveler shook his head, watching the pickup dwindle in the distance. "No. We need the fuel they left here. If we go after 'em, there's too much chance somebody'll come along and cop it. Let's salvage what we can here."

They finished the roadrats who weren't quite dead and buried Jamaica Jack under a cairn of stones.

The dead roadrats they left for the ants.

They found four cans of gas in one of the roadrats' vehicles and siphoned more from the other two. They scavenged what they could from the cars—tools, a few parts that could be adapted for the van, ammo, water, canned foodstuffs—and then set them afire, in case the queen should return.

All this took an hour. At the end of the hour, Traveler said, "Let's hit the road. We'll eat on the way."

"Uh, Traveler . . ."

"Yeah?"

"There's the girl."

Cursing, Traveler looked at the girl sitting in the shade of the Meat Wagon. Link had crowbarred her shackles apart while Traveler had been preoccupied with salvaging. She wore a long man's shirt and a pair of cutoffs she'd found in the trunk of one of the cars. Clothes were tradable loot, too. Even dressed, she looked great. And, dark-skinned, she reminded Traveler achingly of Jan.

"Okay?" Traveler said resigned. "We'll capture a car along the way. She can take it, drive back to Drift."

"And get captured again and enslaved on the way. Or worse."

101

"Look, Link, this gig is tough enough—"

"Have you seen the welts on her, man? The bruises? She's got two cracked ribs from that bitch. She's starving, she—"

"All right, all right, goddamnit, all right!"

Link looked at him. "You usually ain't so . . . Don't lose your temper so much, man. What's eating you?"

Traveler nodded, "You're right. Something's eating me. How many people have we killed in the last forty-eight hours? I don't mind popping caps at roadrats for a purpose but . . . I mean, chasing after this gold . . . I can't get over the feeling that it's bullshit. That it's the kind of futile bullshit that burned up the world. . . . I can't quite explain . . ."

"That's okay man," Link said, grinning. "That's the longest speech you made since I've known you. Damn. You don't have to say nothing else for a week."

Traveler snorted, then laughed.

The girl looked at him with big frightened eyes. He seemed crazy to her.

He shook his head at her and smiled. "You're going to be okay. We're not going to leave you out in the desert."

She smiled back tentatively and looked at Link. He translated. Her smile widened. She stood and moved toward Traveler as if she wanted to thank him—and then swayed, had to put out a hand to steady herself against the van.

"She's weak," Link said. "They didn't feed her much."

"We'll feed her on the way. . . . How come you speak Spanish?"

"I grew up in Spanish Harlem. My old man was black, my mama was Puerto Rican."

102

"That right? You a P.R.? I'm lucky you didn't steal my fucking van."

"Lucky is right," Link said, helping the girl into the van. "And not a word of gratitude for saving your white ass."

"You're lucky I don't fire you for getting there late," Traveler said, starting the van.

They drove back onto the road and into another blazing desert day.

They drove an hour before the girl—Rosalita, it turned out—said something warningly in Spanish from the back. Traveler looked over his shoulder. She'd been looking out the rear window slit.

"What'd she say, Link?"

"She said someone is following us. And they're gaining on us."

10

Deathgate

"How many?" Traveler asked.

Link spoke to Rosalita. She replied in Spanish. He translated, "Two or three cars. She can't tell."

Traveler reached out his window, wiped dust off the side mirror. He could see them, now and then, just glimpsing the vibrating images of two metallic notches against the horizon, a quarter mile behind. "I make out two. Don't think either one is the pickup. The queen cunt's probably following out in the desert."

"Maybe just more . . . 'prospectors.' "

"Yeah. Can Rosalita shoot?"

"Says she can shoot a pistol or a light rifle."

"There's a .22, bolt action, in the gun crate. Box of shells. She'll probably have to use it before the day's out."

Link climbed in back, found the gun, and began to load it for her. She took it from him and used the oily rag and the wire in the crate to clean it, tsk-tsking over the rifle's condition. She loaded it expertly and checked the sights. Link watched her with pleasure. She smiled shyly at him. He reached out to take her hand—and she drew back, afraid, eyes widening.

Link raised a hand to signify *It's okay. Nobody's going to touch you if you don't want to be touched.* Then he came back up front, muttering, "That roadrat cow's got Rosalita bad scared. Maybe ruined her."

"Give her some time," Traveler said.

The Deathgate Hills were looming ahead. Cattle Ivory Flats were nearly at an end. The road began to rise, twisting through a landscape that rose like ocean swells, long low ripples, around them. The grade was steeper; Traveler had to shift down. Any steeper and he'd kick it back into four-wheel drive. The right side of the road soon fell away, dropping sheer to jagged avalanche-refuse below. Thorny, bitter vegetation grew on the stony hillsides along with the occasional pine tree. Now and then a lizard darted from a sunning rock at their approach.

The sun beat down mercilessly. The interior of the Meat Wagon became an oven. There was little relief from the wind of their movement now; they were climbing at barely thirty mph.

And then Link, who held the golden platter in his lap, said, "That's it, that's the turn—see that big, lightning-blasted stump? Take the right."

The road forked here, the one on the left climbing higher, the one on the right of the blasted stump leveling out, continuing west.

"What do we look for now?" Traveler asked, as he passed a jug of water over his shoulder to Rosalita.

"If I read the map right, we continue this way for a

good distance, around this small mountain. We look for a rock with a body chained to it. Behind that rock will be the trail leading up into the hills. Follow the trail. He left markers . . ."

"He left more than markers," Traveler said. "The old vulture probably left bombs, avalanche-triggers, punji pits, crossbow traps, poisoned water, and his pet rattlesnakes."

"Traveler man, I do believe you're getting cynical. Where's the fresh-faced, naïve kid I usedta know?"

"Fuck off. . . . They still on our tail?"

Link climbed in back for a look. "Yeah. . . . Shit, they're movin' in!"

Traveler rubbed dirt from his mirror and peered into it, made out two vehicles running close, side by side, on the narrow road. There was just enough room for two cars in the width of the dirt road. The one on the left had probably been a black Lincoln Continental. It was hard to tell now; it was heavily armored with slabs of scrap metal, its upper half removed and replaced with a turret of clumsily welded iron slabs, firing slits cut in it for a mortar tube or grenade launcher and a light machine gun. The car on the right had probably been an Impala. It was flashier than the other car. A chrome dorsal fin had been added to the top of the cab; the grill of the Impala had been remade to resemble shark's jaws like some of the old W.W. II fighter aircraft, but this car's twisted designer had gone one step further and put some real teeth on his creation. Mounted on the grill was a contrivance of springs and steel teeth that looked like a huge bear trap, running the width of the front of the car. All the guy riding shotgun had to do was jerk a cable and these toothy steel plates would smash down on the ramming bumper, and in gnashing shut bite off anything that fell between their two-foot steel teeth.

The cars gunned closer, gaining on Traveler.

"They're highwaymen," Traveler said. "I know the cars. Seen 'em around Drift."

In the parlance of Traveler's time, highwaymen were pirates of the road who worked out of the less scrupulous settlements, went out at intervals to steal from people using the road—or to steal the people themselves, who were sold as slaves to the Glory Boys. Highwaymen were a cut or two above roadrats. They tended to have wives and children and, too, highwaymen were not murderous drug-crazed madmen.

They were simply murderous.

The three vehicles shrieked around a tight curve in the road, first Traveler and then the highwaymen, one dropping back so they could both take the curve more easily.

"They're a team," Traveler decided aloud, watching them drive. "They work together. . . ."

The road straightened out. They were in for a long, straight stretch.

And it would be here that they'd . . .

"They're making a play for it!" Link confirmed, looking out the back firing slit.

The two cars were only forty feet behind now, and closing. The turreted Lincoln pulled ahead. There was a man in the turret, another below in the driver's seat, a third man in back. The third man stood up to fire a rifle at the Meat Wagon.

Rosalita pushed Link aside and thrust her .22 through the firing slit. She took only a moment to aim. The little rifle kicked, and the man standing in the back of the Lincoln fell back, a neat hole in the center of his forehead.

"Damn, the woman can shoot!" Link burst out.

She cocked the rifle and fired again. But the armor on the car protected the driver from her next shots.

"That's all for here," Link said. "That gun's too light for this. Head up front and—Oh, I forgot." He repeated it in Spanish, and she took the rifle up front.

Traveler was steadily accelerating, trying to pull ahead, but the road was bumpy, treacherous, sometimes unexpectedly narrowed where its edge had crumbled away. If he went too fast, he wouldn't see the narrow place before he hit it. And they'd plunge off the road, into space, and into death.

The speedometer read 50, 55, 60 . . .

The van hit a pothole and leaped, came down teeth-jarringly hard, and he fought the wheel for control, the tires skating . . . the cliff's edge loomed up. And then the tires bit down, and he regained control, veered away from the edge.

"What the hell you doing, Traveler, playing chicken with those rocks down there?" Link demanded, as he clung to a rack on the van's wall to keep from falling.

"Can't go any faster and control the van on this road," Traveler grated, still fighting to keep control.

"If we can't get away from the bastards," Link said, "we'll have to take the fight to the enemy. . . ."

He stuck the AR15 through the gun-slit and squeezed off a burst at the Lincoln. The rounds whined off the armor around the turret.

The turret-man was placing something Link couldn't quite make out in a jar that was tied to the end of a spear in place of a spearhead. Then he stuck the spear in a harpoon launcher, reached out with a piece of flint and a metal bar, began to strike sparks. Gas-soaked rags on the outside of the jar caught fire—and now Link saw that the jar was filled with gas too.

The man in the turret pulled a lever, and the harpoon gun fired, launching the spear—directly at Link's face.

"Shit!" Link yelled, drawing back from the firing slit. The projectile struck the door and the back of the van burst into flames. Flame licked through the slit and began to fill the van with smoke. Link swore and stuffed the hole with a wet rag. The flame streamed out behind the van, flapping like an oily orange flag in the wind.

The shark-car gunned closer, closer, passing the turreted car, its mechanical mouth creakily opening, the jagged steel teeth gleaming in the sunlight, light glancing off the chromium shark fin on the cab-top.

Link unlocked one of the back doors. He had to. The flame had burned out on the doors but spread to oily areas on the underside of the rear bumper. It just might find its way to the fuel line. . . .

Link grabbed a leather skin of water, ripped its cork out and leaned out the door to slosh water on the flame licking up the rear bumper.

The flame sizzled resentfully, went flickeringly out. He held on to the door handle with one hand, leaned out further to make sure the fire was snuffed—and then Traveler hit a bump.

The Meat Wagon bounced and Link was wrenched outward, losing his foot hold in the van's interior, dropping the water skin, instinctively flailing . . .

And he found himself hanging onto the door with

110

both hands, as it swung back and forth, clanging, over the right rear wheel.

He let his feet droop and was nearly torn from his hold when they brushed the road. At 60 mph the road seemed to try to snatch him away from the van.

He jerked back up, clung awkwardly to the door, struggling to force the door back into place. But his weight acted as a counterbalance, holding the door open. The wind pushed against him, trying to tear him from his hold, the car bounced and shivered, and his fingers were going numb trying to hold on. And then, over the thunder of the engines and the roar of the wind, he heard a rapacious *clang* just behind him.

He looked over his left shoulder, saw the monstrous metal jaws cranking open again, gaping for the sole purpose of taking a bite out of him.

He stared in horror at the grotesque machine and willed his limbs to work, pulling himself up onto the frame of the door, fighting wind and gravity and the pain in his fingers. He let go of the door handle on the inside with one hand, holding the one on the outside with the other and clamping the door between his feet; with his free hand he grabbed the rim at the top edge of the van and pulled himself up. Just as the metal teeth clanged shut, inches from his left leg.

Link scrambled blindly up into the even fiercer wind pressure on the roof of the van. He crawled ahead, holding on spread-eagled, trying to reach the easier hand hold of the machine gun mounts.

The wind battered at his face and smashed an insect on his teeth.

*   *   *

Traveler shouted over his shoulder, "What the fuck's happening back there, Link?"

The Chicano girl jabbered at him excitedly in Spanish, but he couldn't make it out. She was upset about something. That much he was sure of.

He felt a blast of cool air from behind, risked a look over his shoulder.

Link was gone. And one of the back doors was open.

And then he heard the banging from the roof.

Was that Link—? Or had some highwayman climbed on?

He heard another sound. A grinding, crunching, squealing sound, like metal biting into metal. That's exactly what it was. He looked over his shoulder. The shark-car had bitten down on the back of the van, holding on at the right rear bumper.

The van yawed, fishtailing.

"The guy's a damn fool!" Traveler muttered. "We'll both go over the edge this way!" But the car hung on like a bulldog, braking to slow the van down. Traveler slowed, cursing.

The turret-car drew up alongside, its turret swiveling to point the light machine gun at Traveler's windshield.

And then something black fell from the sky.

It was Link, leaping down at the turret, landing like a cat atop it, bending to wrench the machine gun muzzle back so it spit its hellfire harmlessly into the air.

The three vehicles swerved on the road till it looked like they'd go off at the curve coming up. . . . Metal squealed under metal teeth . . . tires complained . . .

Traveler cursed, "Fuck this!" He'd had enough.

He stomped on the brakes.

The two interlocked cars skidded—and stopped. The

112

turret-car, Link atop it struggling with the gunman, sped on without them. Traveler snatched up his crossbow, already cocked and loaded, and his Colt, and climbed over the back seat just in time to meet the man climbing in the rear door from the shark-car.

He was a bulky man with a mane of shaggy black hair and beard and an animal snarl showing off a sharklike mouthful of teeth. He wore denim and bandoliers, in the fashion of highwaymen, and he carried a long-barreled Smith and Wesson revolver, which he leveled at Traveler a second too late. Traveler fired the crossbow, but the man moved at the same instant, and the arrow went into the meat of his right shoulder. The highwayman dropped the gun, his face contorted with pain; but as Traveler raised the Colt, the man recovered himself and charged, rushing in past the gun muzzle, knocking Traveler flat on his back in the bed of the van.

Traveler struggled against the big road pirate's oppressive weight, returning a glare for the hate-filled glare in the man's red-rimmed eyes. He dropped the crossbow. The highwayman closed his fingers around Traveler's throat, and Traveler used his freed hand to grab the shaft of the arrow in his assailant's shoulder, twisting it cruelly in the wound.

The big man howled with pain and grabbed at the hand that was torturing him—which gave Traveler room enough to bring the Colt up and fire point blank in the big man's face. Flesh and blood and bone exploded and spattered Traveler's cheeks; he tasted the man's blood on his lips.

Traveler rolled the corpse off him. He heard a gunshot behind him and turned toward the front seat. Rosalita held a smoking .22 rifle. Another highwayman

113

had forced the side door open, and was now staggering back with a .22 bullet in his belly. He fell backwards off the roadside cliff, tumbled screaming to the rocks below.

There was a creaking sound from the rear, Traveler turned and saw the shark-car releasing its hold on the Meat Wagon, backing up.

Traveler shouted in wordless fury and, his face smeared with blood, his eyes wild, smoking pistol in his hand, he leaped from the back of the Meat Wagon and onto the hood of the shark-car. The driver swung left and shifted into drive, accelerated past the van as Traveler—fighting to keep his balance—moved slowly along the hood toward the driver.

The car picked up speed, the driver jerking the wheel now and then to try and dislodge the invader.

Traveler threw himself onto the windshield, pressed the muzzle to it, and shouted, "Pull over!"

The driver angrily shook his head.

Traveler knew if he shot the driver the car just might go over the cliff.

It would be irrational. Stupid. Foolish. But they'd fucked up his car.

He yelled, "See you in hell, asshole!"

And pulled the trigger twice.

The windshield shattered inward, bullets and broken glass turning the driver's face into a mask of raw meat. The car swerved toward the cliff-edge.

Traveler leaped free, saw the road rushing at him, wondered which bones he'd break, and then a fist of stone and clay smashed the wind out of him, knocked the gun from his hand, and everything spun.

The spinning stopped, a long sickening time later—

just seconds, but it had seemed to take an hour—and, groggily, he sat up.

Tire tracks led to the cliff-edge and over. The shark-car was gone.

He hurt. His head hurt from the blows the Spike had given him that morning. He ached from a dozen bruises he'd picked up in the last ten minutes. *And where was Link?*

He looked around—then froze.

The turret-car was only ten feet away. Link lay on the ground beside it, dazed, trying to get up, blood streaming from the reopened wound on his neck and a fresh scalp wound.

The driver of the turret-car was standing beside it, standing over Link, cocking a pistol.

"Link!" Traveler said hoarsely, getting to his feet.

He saw a man behind the machine gun in the turret-car. But his head was twisted to one side, skewed wrongly. Link had broken the guy's neck. But while Link was doing that, the driver had stopped the car. And he'd knocked Link off it, hitting him from behind. And now the bastard had the jump on them both.

The driver looked from Link to Traveler, trying to decide which one he would shoot first.

Traveler looked around for the Colt, saw it lying near the cliff-edge, coated in dust.

Shouldn't let a gun get that dirty, he thought, as he was about to be shot down.

But the highwayman looked up, past Traveler, in terror, and for the second time that day the Meat Wagon came to Traveler's rescue. This time Rosalita was at the wheel.

Traveler heard it rumbling near, turned to see it, and

115

thought: It's as if the van itself is coming to save me, somehow arranging to get itself a driver when it needs one. Like it possesses them.

And the van roared straight for them. Thirty feet away and coming fast.

Link gathered himself together, using the gunman's distraction, and leaped from the ground at the man's waist, bowling him over.

Traveler trotted over and stepped on the driver's gun-wrist.

"Please, mister!" the highwayman said, as the van pulled up, grinding to a halt just four feet away.

He was just a kid. Eighteen or so. Slender. Matted blond hair, scraggly blond beard, sunburnt face, frightened blue eyes.

Link grabbed the pistol, sat up, straddling the boy, pointed it at his face.

"Wait—" Traveler began. Wanting to let him go.

But Link had pulled the trigger, and the boyish face was smashed open, the brains mingled with the dust of the road.

Link looked groggily up, his face smeared with dust and blood, his expression blurred from pain and fatigue. "You . . . you say something, man?"

Traveler shook his head.

11

The Golden Trail

They left the turret-car splayed diagonally across the road in a narrow turn, firmly in the way. They set it on fire, and turned their backs on it. The body of the golden-haired boy burned in the car's back seat.

The boy was no good at killing, Traveler thought. If he had been, Link and I would both be dead by now. Twenty years ago he'd probably have been an English major.

Now there weren't any English majors because there weren't any colleges.

But there was still gold.

And men still killed for it. As long as there are men and gold, Traveler thought, there will be murder.

They drove the slightly charred Meat Wagon up the road and around the mountain, looking for the boulder that marked the treasure trail.

Traveler several times made out the tracks of the

dragster. He was surprised the flimsy-looking vehicle had made it so far.

Traveler was driving. Every time they hit a pothole the Meat Wagon bounced, painfully jarring Traveler's bruises, his cracked ribs. Link was lying in the back. Rosalita had cleaned the dirt from him, cleansed his wounds with alcohol, and bandaged him. He lay with his head in her lap. Asleep or pretending to be.

The van nosed around a long curve, and the road began to ascend again. Traveler shifted down. The day had worn on; the light was like a threadbare yellow cloth.

Traveler was daydreaming about showers and clean motel rooms, extinct luxuries, when they rounded another corner and came to a sort of cleft in the hillside; the road bellied out here, on the left, across from the cliff-edge.

They'd come east and south from the site of the last fire fight. The hill occluded the sun here; a long, blue-gray shadow fell across the cleft and deepened within it. Traveler pulled off the road below the cleft. At the place where the cleft met the road shoulder, an immense pyramidal stone stood, a chunk of granite. A badly decomposed body was chained to it. Big iron chains. The body was spreadeagled faceup on the upper face of the pyramid shape; it had gone gray as the stone it was stretched on, and nearly as desiccated, and its few remaining rags of clothing were almost indistinguishable from the flaps of skin hanging torn around the open wounds in its chest. It stared sightlessly at them with empty eye sockets. Ants crawled in and out of the nostrils.

"That's what I like to see," Link said, climbing into the front. "A good omen."

Traveler put the Meat Wagon in park and got cautiously out, looking up at the hillsides, half expecting someone to take a shot at him.

The steep hillsides overhead were shadowy, bereft of movement.

There was no sound but the crunch of their bootsteps, which echoed with ghostly ringing from the natural amphitheater rising around them. The air was heavy with imminence.

There was no sign of the dragster. Traveler looked at the ground, but it was too stony here to take a clear impression of tracks.

They walked all the way around the thirty-foot stone, expecting to see the dragster on the other side. But there was no one, nothing but stone and shadow and lichen.

"What you think happened to them?" Link asked, in a whisper. He didn't want his voice to echo.

Traveler shrugged. "I can guess. My guess is they went up the road a ways, found a place to hide their car, then hoofed it back here fast. And they're on the trail ahead of us."

Link nodded. "It'd be crazy to leave the car here. . . ."

The woman said something in Spanish. Traveler looked quizzically at Link.

Link said, "She says we're fools to stand around here like this. The other treasure hunters could be hidden up above, ready to kill us with sniping."

There was nothing to be said to that.

They went back to the van and got in. They drove

down the road a half-mile farther and found a side road leading downward into a patch of scrub oaks. The dragster was nowhere to be seen—but Traveler felt sure it was camouflaged nearby.

They parked in the shelter of the oaks, behind a screen of Joshua trees and cacti, and ate another meal in the back of the van.

Traveler felt drained. The food was tasteless in his mouth—which was maybe just as well.

Traveler rested, his back against the interior wall of the van. He found his eyes straying to the crate, close beside him, in which he kept his few mementos. He opened it with one hand, listlessly, and looked at the yellowing snapshot of himself with Orwell, Margolin, and Hill in El Hiagura. They wore fatigues, bush hats, camouflage dappling on everything.

Margolin was boyish, blond, slender . . . Maybe that was what had bothered him, at least in part, about killing that highwayman on the road. The kid had looked a lot like Margolin had, fifteen years before. But Margolin had been good at killing. . . . And Orwell. Big, a little round-faced, black, slightly crooked sunglasses. . . . And Hill, the lean, long-nosed eccentric, with his crooked smile and his feathered serpent tattoo and his forked beard and his twirling waxed mustaches and his crinkled blue eyes. And his lethal reflexes.

Their friendship had been forged and reforged under fire.

Looking at them now was some kind of unthinking ritual, he realized. And he realized, too, that he didn't expect to come out of this one alive.

*   *   *

120

"You think she'll stay put?" Traveler asked, as they trudged away from the van.

"Rosalita? She didn't seem thrilled with the idea. But yeah, she'll stay put. And she'll protect the van better than all the booby traps in the world could. Woman's a living booby trap."

"That a pun? Never mind. Hey—you hear something?"

Both men froze, listening. There was a faint crackling sound in the brush behind them.

They were in a stand of gnarled oaks. The oaks were parched, thin, none wider than two feet through the trunk. Not much cover. But Traveler and Link each stepped behind one, apiece, turned sideways to minimize themselves as targets. Traveler carried the AR15, Link the heavier AR180.

They were in a trough between two long moraines of rock; there was stiff, straw-yellow grass underfoot. Around the base of the outcroppings were thick patches of dead-blue sage.

"Maybe just a rabbit," Link said, a second before a bullet tore a chunk of his tree away.

"What kind of ordnance that rabbit using?" Traveler asked, ducking back.

"Sounds like he's got an assault rifle on semiauto in his furry little paws," Link said.

Traveler risked a look through the crotch-space between a branch and the trunk. There was a flash in the shade of the sage, about fifty feet away, and the branch beside his face flew apart, fell away from the tree. He ducked back, swearing, then knelt, preparing to lean out for a burst at the place the muzzle flash had come from. . . .

And a voice behind him said, "Drop the guns or I'll paste your brains to those trees."

Traveler hesitated. He was damned if he did and damned if he didn't. If he dropped the gun, the guy would be free to shoot him. Or torture him and then shoot him, if it was a roadrat. If he went for it, chances were the guy would blow him apart before he so much as turned around.

"Don't think about it," the voice said. "Do it. Do it, and you'll live."

Traveler glanced at Link. Link shrugged as if to say, "We got nothing to lose."

Traveler dropped his rifle. Link dropped his.

"Now turn around."

Traveler turned slowly around. The man facing him, twenty feet away, was holding an HK91 assault rifle. He wore fatigues and crossed bandoliers over a bare chest. He was a lean man in goggles, with a bristle of brown hair and . . .

And a forked beard. And waxed mustaches. And a tattoo on his forearm of the Aztec god Quetzalcoatl, the feathered serpent.

"Where you find the mustache wax, Hill?" Traveler asked. There was just the faintest tremor in his voice.

The man stiffened, then turned a stare at Traveler.

He reached up with one hand and pushed the goggles back on his head.

"I know you," he said. But there was no friendliness in his voice. Just puzzlement.

Traveler took a step nearer him. "Frank . . ."

Hill snapped the gun up to point at Traveler's chest. He'd gone rigid, but rock-still. "Don't you move."

A voice chilling as the rattle of a rattlesnake.

There was a crisp sound of approaching footsteps through the grass from behind. A tall, slender, wirily muscular man with matted blond hair and a tanned, boyish face moved between Link and Traveler, turned to face them. His rifle was identical to his partner's. Both men had absurd pandalike rings of dust around their eyes from the goggles.

He looked less boyish when you looked at him up close. There was a twitch in one cheek and a desperate wildness in his eyes.

But it was Margolin, all right.

"Margolin," Traveler said. "What's happening, Bill? You get the crotch-rot again lately? Remember that time you got the Fiendish Fungus from that whore in San Salvador?"

Margolin swallowed, his Adam's apple bobbing on his long neck. He took a step back. He pointed the gun at Traveler.

"Who is he, Frank?" Margolin's voice was like the rustling of dried leaves. The twitch redoubled its twitching.

"I don't know . . ." Hill's eyes were dilated.

Both men had their guns pointed at Traveler. Their fingers hovered on the hair triggers. One nervous twitch, one hysterical reaction, and something more than bullets would be triggered. Irony would be triggered—the irony of a man shot down by the friends he'd searched years to find.

Traveler's mouth was dry. "Hill, Margolin . . . It's *Paxton*. Kiel Paxton."

"He's lying, Frank," Margolin said raspily. "Kiel's dead."

"It could be a desert devil," Hill said in a maddeningly reasonable voice. "Didn't I tell you that devils live in the desert, Bill? Sure I did. Remember we read it in the New Testament. They tempted Jesus when he walked in the desert. They live out there because it's Hell on Earth. And they know what we think and what we remember. They could take on the shape of Kiel Paxton. . . ."

Margolin nodded. "A devil. A shape-changer."

They've gone mad, Traveler realized. Mad together. Driven mad by the dose of NT77 we got. The main effects of the stuff probably wore off years ago. But they didn't have the serum to get them through like I did.

"You know I almost don't blame you for believing I'm a desert devil," Traveler said. "I've seen things. . . . Things that strange." And it was true. He had. "But I'm not the Paxton you remember. I'm Paxton the way he would be if he'd aged fifteen years."

"The devils are clever," Hill admitted.

The rifle remained rock-still in his hands, pointed at Traveler's belly.

"Traveler, what the fuck—" Link began.

Traveler shook his head at Link. "Let me handle it."

"What did he call him?" Margolin said. "Not Paxton."

"It's a nickname. People call me Traveler now."

"Traveler," Hill said thoughtfully. "I heard of him. They say he drives a fine black van. . . . And you got one. But . . ."

Hill raised his rifle to his shoulder. "It's a devil. If we shoot it and it lives, we know it's a devil!"

"But what if it dies—and it was Kiel?" Hill pointed out, to Traveler's relief.

"Frank," Traveler said, licking his lips. "Frank, buddy—how about this: you put down that piece, Margolin keeps his, and you and I have a little wrestling match. . . . Remember? Like we used to have?"

Hill cocked his head to one side. He grinned and laid the gun down in the grass.

"Frank, what you doing?" Margolin said, his voice rising an octave.

"I'm gonna wrestle with the devil," Hill said, his wolfish grin widening.

And he rushed at Traveler.

Traveler ran at him—and ducked. He reached beneath the other man, grabbed his ankles firmly, and kept plunging ahead, throwing Hill completely over him. Hill landed heavily on his back. But he was up in a second, turning to face him, laughing with joy. "I think it might be him, Bill! That's a dirty, sneaking, low-down trick like Kiel woulda used!"

He swung hard at Traveler and connected. Traveler took it on the right side of his jaw. Pain rang through his head and vibrated shrilly in the injury the Spike had given him like a vibration in the crack on the Liberty Bell. He staggered backwards, shook himself, managed to sidestep the charging madman. Then he moved in close behind him, cocked his arm, waiting for him to turn. Hill turned, and Traveler gave him a screaming right hook to the jaw.

Hill fell on his ass. He stared into space for a moment. Then his eyes lit up. "It's him!" he shouted. "It's really Kiel! No wimp of a devil could hit like that! That was a *man* hitting!"

"Ki . . . Kiel?" Margolin stuttered. "I'm . . . it's . . . what?"

But Hill had rushed to embrace Traveler, and the two men stood together, hugging, laughing, and finally Margolin had to accept it. He dropped his gun and went to them, and three men hugged.

"Damn, I feel left out," Link said dryly.

"Well come on, Link!" Traveler shouted, forgetting himself in his relief.

"No way, girls," Link said. "I figured out my sexual preference years ago."

"Hey, fuck off, Link!" Traveler said, laughing, as the three men separated.

There were tears in Margolin's eyes. "You—Vallone told us you were dead!"

"Vallone?" Traveler's eyes narrowed. "When was that?"

"Ten years ago. He tried to recruit us. Then he tried to take us for slaves. The same fucker. I'm gonna get him one of these days," Hill said.

"Sorry," Traveler said. "You can't. I already did." He smiled at the memory. "I got him good."

Traveler looked at Hill. "That was you guys in the dragster?"

Hill nodded. "You know, the reason we didn't just kill you now, when we coulda . . . And the reason we saved you from those roadscums was Bill here. . . . Bill has visions. He . . . gets these pictures. And we always found that if we follow what he dreams, we have luck. We get through. He saw this black van in a dream, and—"

"Yeah," Margolin interrupted excitedly. Boyish again. "Yeah, I had a dream of this little bald-headed guy in a monk's robe—I mean a Buddhist monk. And he had a Siamese cat big as a mountain. And he had a toy of your van, he was letting it run around his feet, like a kid playing with a toy car, and he said to me, he said, 'This car will bring you luck. Find it and keep it from harm.' So we was going to keep you prisoner, like a good luck charm. . . . What's the matter?"

Traveler was looking off toward the cleft, frowning.

"I heard it too," Hill said. His senses had been razored by the NT77 the way Traveler's had. "Sounded like a truck engine, up the road. . . . Hey—*the gold!*"

12

The Golden Trail to Murder

"What we ought to do when we get the gold," Margolin was saying, as they trudged up the path to the road, "is buy a boat, right? A yacht. And sail around the world and find some civilization, somewhere. You know? What you think, Kiel?"

"Good plan," Paxton-Traveler said, when Hill gave him a look that said *Humor the kid.* The two freebooters had accepted Traveler and Link completely. There was an unspoken understanding that the gold would be shared between the four of them. Once, Margolin spoke to Link and called him Orwell.

Orwell was the only member of the team not present—and like Link he'd been black.

Link had raised his eyebrows but said nothing. He seemed to sense that both men were damaged—but loyal to those they chose as friends.

The four men stopped short of the road and cut back along it, moving parallel, back toward the cleft, threading through the brush along the steep slope. One foot higher than the other, it was awkward going. But they'd done the same for miles in worse terrain, in a dozen lethal jungles.

Traveler felt good, and bad as hell, both at once.

It was miraculous, finding his friends again. A miraculous coincidence—if coincidence it was. Margolin had had a dream of Shumi, the wandering Buddhist mystic whose path had crossed and recrossed Traveler's, and whose fate seemed intertwined with Traveler's. It was all too likely that Shumi had a hand in the miraculous reunion. Traveler didn't like the feeling of being manipulated. But when you've had a whole civilization pulled out from under you, the world turned upside down overnight, you learned to accept the fact that life just isn't interested in any one individual's personal preferences.

But still he ached, still he chafed at the mission itself. It seemed wrong, a fool's errand. But the gold . . . Gold could still buy things, even now. Gold could change his life.

But the catch was, he was going to have to kill for it, again and again, till he was choked from killing. And, in the end, he'd probably have to die for it.

And a corpse doesn't give a damn about a gold coffin.

Traveler worried about Hill and Margolin. They were both a bit cracked, especially Margolin. They were unpredictable. They might do anything in a fire fight. . . .

The four men halted just below the lip of the road across from the corpse-marked boulder at the entrance to the golden trail.

"You guys get a chance to recon the trail?" Traveler asked Hill.

Hill shook his head. "Except I'm fairly sure there's only one way up for miles around—up that crack in the mountain. Looks like that trail is the only way. Which smells like an ambush."

Traveler nodded. "What about this—we split up, me and Link go in first, you and Margolin cover us—"

"No!" Margolin was distressed. "No, they—" He turned to Hill. "We'll lose him again! They'll kill him! Let's go in at the same time but in two teams, Frank! Them on one side, us on the other, and we'll cover each other!"

Hill looked questioningly at Traveler. Traveler gave the thumbs-up, then looked at Link. Link shrugged and hefted his AR180 assault rifle. He was ready for anything.

Traveler checked his AR15, then nodded to himself and moved off through the brush to the left. Hill and Margolin went to the right. They'd clamp the trail entrance between them.

If Hill and Margolin could be counted on . . .

"You sure about those two?" Link asked in a whisper, as they climbed toward the road.

"No," Traveler said.

"Oh, well then, I feel better," Link said dryly.

Traveler braced himself on the trunk of a bush growing crookedly out from the hillside and lifted his head above the edge of the road.

Across the dusty dirt road a blackened convoy truck—its paint blistered, its windshield shot out—stood beside the boulder. A Glory Boy sentry stood guard at both ends. The truck stood with its tailgate to the boulder. Now and then the sentry at that end glanced up at the corpse spread-eagled on the boulder and then looked quickly away.

Link moved up beside Traveler. "I don't see anybody else. . . . That truck look familiar, man?"

Traveler nodded. "It's all that's left of the convoy we blew off down on the flats. Bound to be more of them up on the trail. . . ." He looked to his right, saw Hill about a hundred feet down. Traveler caught Hill's eye; he pointed west, then made a circular motion with one finger, followed by a throat-cutting gesture. Hill nodded.

"What was that all about?" Link asked.

"Told him to go down the road so he can cross out of sight of the sentries, then come back. We'll take the guards out quietly. Don't want to alert the fake patriots up on the trail."

Traveler led Link to the left, still below the edge of the road, till the bulk of the pyramidal boulder stood between them and the truck. Then they climbed up and crossed, sprinting as quietly as possible to the boulder. Traveler whispered terse instructions in Link's ear, and then began to climb up on the boulder.

Link waited till Traveler was twenty feet overhead, close beside the corpse—and then he picked up a piece of gravel and tossed it against the boulder. The sentry ambled around the rock, M16 in hand, not particularly worried. It had been a small sound, and he'd probably assumed it was a lizard, but checking on it gave him something to do. Just routine.

Until someone dropped on him from above, knocked him flat on his stomach, smashed his face into the dirt so he couldn't cry out, and cut his throat.

The sentry at the front of the truck heard the scuffle and frowned. He switched his M16's safety off and, half-crouched, moved softly around the truck, calling, "Marv, you okay?"

He was just about to shout for help, deciding that something must have happened to Marv since he didn't reply, when steely fingers clamped over his mouth, another hand jerked his rifle from his grasp, and yet another slashed through his windpipe with a razor-sharp knife.

Traveler and Hill each took an M16 from their respective victims, and an extra clip, strapping the rifles over their backs to supplement their handheld firepower. There was a good chance they'd run out of ammo on the trail ahead.

The trail zigzagged up through the cleft, like a staircase in a stairwell. But there were no steps. There were places where the shale was loose underfoot, and places where the climb was almost straight up. There were outcroppings of rock at intervals hiding what was above, and places where the cleft screwed itself into the mountainside, became a kind of crooked chute that covered what was above no matter where you stood below to try and see.

They paused about seventy-five feet up the trail, looking down at the truck and the corpse chained to the rock. Traveler could see the sentry he'd propped up in the cab of the truck behind the wheel in as lifelike a pose as they'd been able to arrange. If more treasure hunters came along, there was a good chance they'd open fire on the propped-up body before they knew it was dead, wasting ammo and alerting people up above.

Margolin took a canteen from his backpack, took a swig from it, and handed it to Traveler. They were in the shade, here, but it was like the shadow inside a furnace chimney. Traveler took a swig and handed it on. And then he pointed. They all turned to look and nodded. Someone had painted an arrow in gold on the rock. It pointed straight up the trail. Traveler wondered where the Old Man in the Hole had gotten the gold paint. He didn't wonder aloud—they'd agreed, down below, to maintain silence here as much as possible. The rock-chute would probably carry voices like a megaphone, and none of them cared to tell the Glory Boys that they were on the way up.

They continued upward, at each bend in the trail pausing, one of them—a different one each time— running ahead to see what was around the blind turn, the others creeping up to give him firepower support if necessary.

At a hundred feet up they encountered a body.

It was a Glory Boy with a wooden spear through his throat. His eyes were focused on horror, and his hands were stiffened in claws at his throat. Traveler looked the body over and decided he hadn't been dead long. The blood was barely dry.

Link looked at him and silently mouthed, "Booby trap."

Another little joke from the Old Man in the Hole.

Traveler found nothing useful on the body and left it as it was.

They moved on, and up. Traveler went ahead now. His eyes searched the rocky, gray-shot earth for telltale signs of traps.

Twenty minutes of climbing passed. His breath was a knife in his lungs; his heart beat loud and forbodingly in his chest. The assault rifle in his hands was heavy and slippery with sweat. The M16 chafed his back. Up above, the chute was knobbed by outcroppings; only the occasional scallop of blue sky showed through.

They climbed on, and the tension grew, every step bringing them closer to confrontation with the enemy—the living enemy and the dead one.

And then the silence was speared by a scream.

And a thumping, crackling sound. Then a growing thunder.

"Avalanche!" Traveler hissed.

They ran back down the trail twenty feet to a big outcropping of granite thrusting five feet out from the chute's wall. The four men pressed against the rock beneath the outcropping, and a half second later a series of basketball-sized boulders came bounding, ricocheting down the chute, whacking into rocks, smashing the softer ones into flinders, rebounding to fall farther down the cleft, smashing again. Any one of those rocks was going fast enough, was big enough, to pulp a man's gut or make paste of his head.

Chips of stone rained down; dust billowed up, choking them.

A rock big as a bushel basket came booming down the natural shaft, spitting fragments of rock wherever it impacted. It bounced from the trail just above them and came whirling straight for their outcropping.

Traveler felt sure it would break the outcropping off, smash it down on them.

The boulder struck; the outcropping above them cracked; the boulder bounded on downward, the outcropping tipped down—and the four men threw themselves aside. The shelf of rock smashed harmlessly down between them, missing Margolin and Link by a hairs-breadth.

The avalanche had subsided to a trickle of gravel and a few larger stones that thumped bruisingly down on their backs and shoulders. And then it stopped completely. The dust began to settle. They paused to take stock. No one was seriously hurt. The weapons were intact.

Traveler looked at the three other men questioningly.

Each one signed that he was willing to go on. Traveler nodded and led the way.

Another hundred feet up they found two Glory Boys crushed by boulders.

One of them was still alive. A boulder sat on his chest, driving splinters of bone through his lungs. Traveler lifted it off. The wounded man coughed up blood and managed, "Hurts. Hurts like hell. . . . Finish me quick, in heaven's name."

"If you'll do us a favor," Traveler whispered. "How many up there?"

"Five more. . . . I don't know if there . . . are others. . . ."

What happened? Booby-trapped rocks?"

The man nodded weakly. "Damn that old . . . man. . . ." His face contorted with agony. "Please . . . end it. . . ."

Traveler said, "Close your eyes, friend." The man screwed his eyes shut, and Traveler pulled his knife and slid it in beneath the cruched ribs and into his heart. The Glory Boy quivered and then went limp in relief, and Traveler almost envied him.

They continued to climb.

Abruptly, the chute came to an end.

The trail moved sharply to the left between two slabs of stone and leveled out. It was a relief to end the climbing, at least for now. But the gold paint marking the way unsettled Traveler. He knew it marked the way to more of the Old Man's treachery.

The trail followed a ravine in the rock just beneath the top of a plateau of some sort, like a furrow etched in a table.

It cut to the right about forty feet ahead. Traveler paused, raising a hand to signal the others. All four men froze.

Traveler had heard noises from around the rock corner. Men speaking in hushed tones; the clank of metal on stone.

Traveler flicked the safety off on his AR15.

He motioned to the others to get down and stay where they were. Then he crept ahead a few feet and, cautiously, looked around the corner.

Thirty feet away, men with milk-white hair stood over their captives, examining captured hardware and pack stores.

One of the Glory Boys lay dead with a razored boomerang lodged in his neck. As Traveler watched, a digman bent to retrieve the boomerang and wiped it on the dead man's jeans. The other four Glory Boys were trussed in the tarred nets. Now and then one of them struggled to get loose, and a digman would give him a resounding kick. "You will be free soon," a digman told his captives. "After your blood flows into the Earthgod, you will be free forever."

There were seven digmen, two of them now hauling the Glory Boys by their ankles to a trapdoor in the earth.

137

Traveler stared at the trapdoor, surprised. Was it cut in solid rock? But maybe it wasn't as solid as it looked, here. There must be caverns below.

Beyond the cluster of men the trail ended at a tumble of boulders. A dead end. But to one side a boulder had been splashily painted with a large gold arrow, pointing into the heap.

The gold . . . was in *there*?

Under four tons of rock?

"The old bastard," Traveler breathed, backing up.

"What's the story?" Link whispered, as the three men huddled around him.

"Digmen," Traveler said. "They got the Glory Boys. They've got a tunnel or something over there. I don't know if it's bullshit, but the markers for the gold are on the other side of the digmen's camp. The digmen are sure to have some kind of way to watch the ground over their hole. We go that way, they'll ambush us."

"There's probably a lot more of them underground," Link said. "The Old Man in the Hole musta made some kind of deal with 'em. Told 'em where to wait along the way for the suckers he set up for this."

"We'll rush them!" Margolin hissed, his face twitching, his eyes bright. "Rush them and kill them all!"

"Bill—the odds are too heavy that way," Traveler said.

But it was as if Margolin hadn't heard. "I'm tired of this! I'm going to kill them!" He turned away from Traveler, began to walk toward the digmen's camp.

Hill nodded solemnly and began to go along with Margolin.

Traveler muttered, "Shit!" and rushed to stand between Margolin and the trail to the digmen's camp.

138

"Bill—if we go this way," he whispered urgently, "we'll get screwed. That ain't teamwork! Remember the teamwork we had in El Hiagura?"

Margolin stood staring dully at the ground. "I remember El Hiagura. I remember the yellow cloud that made shit out of my brain." He looked at Traveler with tears in his eyes, repeating, "I remember, Kiel."

Traveler swallowed. He shook his head. "You're okay, Bill—if you stick with your friends, you'll be okay."

Hill nodded, and touched Margolin on the shoulder. "Yeah. Let's stick with Kiel."

Margolin nodded slowly. "Kiel's the C.O., anyway."

Traveler smiled at him and clapped him on the shoulder. "Good—now listen, buddy—I got another plan. We're almost at the top of the plateau here, right? So we climb up here. We go around, come down behind the digmen's hole. Maybe we don't have to mess with them at all."

Wishful thinking.

13

The Last Laugh

They felt vulnerable, exposed on the plateau top. It was really a sort of flattened moutaintop, rising in humps here and there, creviced, dead as the surface of the moon. The sun was low in the sky, throwing a blunt red-yellow glare over the rocky wasteland.

Was this where the legendary Howard Hughes stashed a treasure? Traveler wondered. Or was the old man lying to us? Maybe the gold he used to make the maps was all he had. . . .

Traveler shrugged. They'd come this far.

They circled the ravine in which the trail lay, coming to the dead end of it in roundabout way, from above, to avoid digman spotters.

Above the tumble of boulders at the end of the trail, Traveler and Link consulted the gold map. The map showed an X over a box with a group of circles in it—that would be the dead end. At the bottom of the map were these words: *At end of trail, find rock marked with gold X, pull lever. Door opens.*

Traveler shook his head at Link. "If we're smart, we turn back now. We pull that lever the shit's gonna come down. I don't know what it'll be—maybe another avalanche, maybe a bomb, I don't know—but it's coming down."

"What shit?" Margolin asked. "What're you talking about?"

"I'm talking about the Old Man's sense of humor," Traveler said. "You saw some examples down there on the trail. Three men dead from the Old Man's booby traps. Then the digmen. The Old Man is sure to have loaded the dice."

"I knew the Old Man," Hill said. "I did business with him more than once. He was a prick. He was a backstabber—but he wasn't a liar. If he said there was a ton of gold in there, it's in there. 'Course, it'd suit him fine if we were all to die before we got to it. . . ."

Link shrugged. "I've got to know. . . . Let's check it out, and we won't do any hasty lever-pulling."

Traveler said, "Let's do it."

They moved belly-down, crawling to the edge of the ravine overlooking the dead end. The trail seemed deserted, now. The traces of the digmen had been covered over. Traveler looked in vain for digmen spotters. Maybe they had a listening tube leading down into the cavern.

But then, who had camouflaged the trapdoors?

He had the answer to that a moment later when they climbed down onto the tumble of boulders, about twenty-five feet above the trail, and came face to face with a digman warrior. The spotter, the camouflager.

This one was *big*. He was armed only with a boomerang and a spear. Traveler didn't want to use the guns

142

till necessary because of the noise. The other men were behind him, and the narrow path across the top of the boulder on which he and the digman stood left no room for anyone to assist him.

Traveler raised the AR15. "Drop your weapons and you won't be hurt!" he hissed.

"You are a lying demon from the upper hells!" the digman replied, flinging the boomerang.

Traveler caught the whirling blade on his rifle barrel, deflecting it into the rocks below. He winced at the clanging sound it made, hoping the other digmen didn't hear it. The gaunt, blue-eyed warrior charged him, jabbing the short spear at Traveler's throat. Traveler snaked aside. The spearpoint cut so close to his neck that the haft burned along his skin.

The digman kept hold of the spear—and yelped with dismay when Margolin, behind Traveler, grabbed the haft as it went over Traveler's shoulder and hissed, "Get down, Kiel!"

Traveler hunched down, and Margolin leaned over him, twisted the warrior off-balance. The man lost his footing and fell sideways, landing twenty feet below on his head. His head smashed and his neck broke.

Margolin tossed the spear aside, and they continued, shinnying down the rocks to the gold arrow at the far side.

The arrow pointed into a passage made by the accidental positioning of fallen rock. It went back into darkness. Margolin drew a candle from his pack and lit it.

"I'm going in," he said, pushing past Traveler.

Traveler looked a plea at Hill. Hill held Margolin

back. "Kiel's the C.O., remember? He decides."
Reluctantly, Margolin nodded.

"I'm going," Traveler said. "You guys follow a good three feet behind me. See anything looks wrong, point at it. Look but don't touch."

He drew his knife and took the candle.

He went into the passage, crouched beneath the low, uneven ceiling, tapping the rocky floor ahead of him with the knife, looking for booby traps.

The candle threw mothlike fragments of light over the grainy, convex surfaces around him. Something scuttled to escape the yellow glow. Candle wax dripped hot on his hands.

Twenty feet back the passage angled right. He turned the corner and saw an old, rusting metal door, six feet away.

He took a step toward it—and a whisper of sound made him throw himself back.

A wooden stake splintered itself on the stone, having whizzed through the spot he'd stood in a moment before.

The Old Man had rightly judged that when the treasure hunter saw the door, he'd forget caution, for a moment. And step on the trigger-rock that launched the spring-tension projectile.

Margolin was leaning over him. "You okay, Kiel?"

"Yeah. . . ." Traveler sat up, found the candle still burning on its side but flickering, threatening to go out. He straightened it up, and it brightened. "Let's try that again," he said. "But you guys move back down the passage while I check this out. No sense we all go if there's another trap." Margolin withdrew. Traveler moved toward the door, once more tapping experimentally with the knife. . . .

144

14

Triumph of the Queen

Traveler stopped, listening.

There were shouts from behind. Link's voice. A rattle of gunfire, echoing harshly to him down the passage. He turned and, still crouched, began to move out through the tunnel. Hill stood at the entrance, silhouetted against the light, his back to Traveler.

Traveler heard the Spike's raspy voice. "Come on out, Traveler, or we shoot the whole bunch of 'em!"

Traveler ground his teeth. It seemed the only way to get rid of the Spike was to kill her. And kill her he would. Somehow.

He took the M16 off his shoulders and stashed it between two rocks, butt outward, hidden in a patch of shadow. Then, carrying the AR15, he shouted, "I'm coming out! I surrender! Hold your fire!"

He emerged from the passageway into the sunlight, tossing the candle aside. The Spike and her single remaining follower stood there. She held a shotgun; the grimy-faced, bearded roadrat held Link's AR180.

"The piece too, pretty-boy," the Spike said. Traveler dropped the rifle.

He was staring at Margolin.

Bill Margolin lay on the ground, blood streaming from a wound in his chest. He breathed liquidly. Hill sat down beside him and took Margolin's head on his lap.

Once he did that, Hill simply stared into space.

Link stood to one side, his arms hanging limp, weaponless. "It was my fault, Traveler," he said. "One of 'em hit me from behind. Stunned me. Dragged me out here. Margolin came out to help me and they gunned him down and . . .." His voice broke. He shrugged and looked away.

"Nobody's fault but this scuzzy cow's here," Traveler said, staring at the Spike.

She laughed in his face, and her laughter stank.

"What'd you do with Rosalita?" the Spike growled.

"She's on her way to Drift," Traveler said. "Listen— you can forget about the gold. I don't think there is any. The Old Man had his laugh on us all. So we're fighting for nothing."

"There's no such thing as fighting for nothing," the Spike said. "Fighting's enough. It's all any of us have left. . . . And don't give me that bullshit about the gold. You're pathetic, trying to keep me out that way. I got a map too. I know where the stuff is. Now stand aside!"

Traveler shrugged. He stood aside.

"Keep a close eye on these shits," the Spike told her roadrat minion.

"But Spike—what about the gold?" he whined, like a little kid. "I wanna see the gold too!"

"Do what I tell you—!"

"Ah, but couldn't we shoot 'em now, huh? Then we could both go in, huh, Spike, couldn't we?"

He was a foot taller than her and built like four sides of beef. But she strode up to him and reached up to slap his face, twice. "Who's the queen of the Wasps?"

"You are, Spike, but—"

"Are you a Wasp?"

"Yeah, Spike, but—"

"Then you take orders from the queen and you don't ask questions!"

"But, ah, Spike, the *go*-old!" There were tears streaming down his face, making the grime run like mascara.

Traveler watched in amazement. Link tensed, figuring this was the time to go for it, and Traveler moved his hand to his belt for his throwing stars, to back Link up.

But the Spike whirled and pointed her shotgun at Link. "Don't even think about it!"

Fury showed in Link's eyes like the far-off flash of a distant lightning storm. But he looked into the double barrels of the shotgun and held himself in check.

Traveler moved his hands away from the shuriken. The time was not yet.

"Now you see what you did, Rugg!" the Spike bellowed. "They almost jumped us!"

"I'm sorry, Spike—"

"Just do what I tell you and you won't have to be sorry! And stop sniveling!"

"I'm sorry, Spike!" he sniveled.

"Now just keep an eye on these losers and when we get the gold, we'll make some knives out of it and we'll cut'em to pieces with it! And we'll take our time with it!"

"That'll be *fun*, Spike!" Rugg said, wiping his eyes with one hand, with the other carefully holding the rifle on Traveler and Link.

"Good." She turned and ducked into the passage. Then she came back out, and picked up the candle. She fumbled in one of her belt's ammo pouches for a tin box in which she kept her precious few matches. "Saved these for seven years!" she said.

"Spike, you always made me start the fires with sparks!" Rugg whined.

"Shut up! These are for special occasions!"

"You guys should be a comedy team," Traveler said.

"Go on, laugh," Spike said, lighting the candle. "And just keep laughing when we skin you alive. And that *ain't* just an expression."

She turned and went into the passage, candle in one hand and shotgun in the other.

Traveler looked at Margolin. Margolin opened his eyes to look at Traveler. He smiled. "I ain't finished yet. I got some fight in me, Kiel. You'll see, Cap'n."

Traveler smiled and nodded.

Link was looking speculatively at Rugg.

Rugg saw the look and took a step back, pointing the rifle at Link. "I know whatcher thinkin'," the roadrat said. "I'm a crybaby. Well maybe I am. But I ain't no pushover! You try anything I'll mow you down!"

"You gonna let that bitch take all the gold for herself?" Link said. "You can't trust her. That bitch—"

"Don't you call my mama a bitch!" Rugg bellowed.

Link and Traveler looked at each other in surprise. "His *mama*?" Traveler said.

148

Link said: "Yo mama!"

"I said don't say nothin about my—" Rugg began, snarling.

"Don't listen to 'em, Rugg!" the Spike said, emerging from the passage. "They're trying to make you mad, get you off guard. . . ." She looked at Traveler. "It almost worked. I almost pulled that lever. But I'm no god-damn fool. I saw that smashed booby-trap stick! You're gonna go in there and pull that lever for me! Get goin'!"

Traveler looked at Link and Hill. He gave a small salute. A good-bye.

And then he bent and went into the passage.

"Wait a minute, take the candle," she said. He turned and took the candle—for a moment the candlelight flickered reflectively in her eyes, like the eyes of a beast. He turned away and went down the passage.

The Spike followed close behind him, prodding him now and then with the shotgun.

Traveler tensed, fighting to control himself. *Your time is coming, you maggot-infested bitch*, he thought.

And my time too, came the afterthought. *The Old Man'll do for both of us*.

They rounded the turn in the passage and came to the metal door. It was just four feet high and three wide, dented and rusty.

If there was gold here, why hadn't the digmen gone for it? Traveler wondered. What do they know that we don't?

He hesitated at the door, looking for a lever.

"It's overhead, in that dark spot," she rasped. "Gowan, gowan! Grab it and pull!"

She shuffled back a step, to avoid whatever booby trap was about to take him out.

He lifted the candle. In a rocky nook overhead was a slot in the stone. Emerging from the slot was a yellowed skeletal arm, and on the arm was a skeletal hand. The skeleton hand had its fingers extended, as if waiting for a handshake.

Traveler had to chuckle. The Old Man had been a card, all right.

He reached up and took the skeleton's hand.

This is it, he thought. Chances are I pull this and another booby trap'll go off. I'll be dead ten seconds from now.

He hesitated. Maybe he should make a play for the shotgun. His chances were slim. But they were better than if he pulled this "lever."

As if she'd read his mind, the Spike shouted, "Hey, Rugg, can you hear me?"

"*I hear you, Spike!*" came the answering shout, muffled.

"If you hear anything funny, like a gunshot or a scuffle, you kill those assholes out there right away! You got me?"

"*I gotcha, Spike!*"

Traveler sighed.

Fuck it, he thought. Go for broke. Pull the handle on the slot machine.

He pulled the skeletal arm down.

And waited for death.

There was a grinding sound, and then a squealing. The door slowly swung inward.

Traveler waited, expecting an explosion, or the ceiling to fall.

Nothing. Silence.

He held the candle out, into the darkened interior of the vault.

The light played teasingly over stacks of gold bullion.

"Holy shit!" he breathed. It looked like real gold, all right. But something was wrong here. Bad wrong. His too sharp senses were screaming a warning.

"Get outta my way!" the Spike hissed, knocking him aside with the shotgun butt.

He grunted and fell over on his side, instinctively raising the candle high to keep it from going out.

She took the candle from him and went into the vault. He heard her sharp intake of breath as she saw the gold. He heard her mutter. "Gold! We did it! Fuck you, Old Man! It's ours now! Spin in your grave! *It's ours!*"

And then the vault door creaked shut, locking into place with a clicking sound that seemed to declare its finality.

15

The Walls Come Tumblin' Down

Traveler moved silently back along the passage. He felt his way in the darkness, making as little noise as possible. After some groping, risking scorpions and rattlers, he found the butt of the M16.

Driven by curiosity, he crept back along the passage to the iron door, M16 in hand. He listened. No sound from inside. That door was thick.

He felt in his shirt pocket, found his own box of matches. He had only one left. He cradled the M16 under his right arm, used his left hand to strike the match. It flared, lighting up the door with a dull red glow.

He pointed the M16 at the door and pulled the lever.

The door didn't open. But something else happened.

The hand moved back into its slot, vanished for a moment, and then emerged again, with something in its palm. He took the something. It was a note.

It said, "If you get out of here real quick, you might

live. The boulders is going to come down real soon. Don't worry about the gold. The chamber is . . ." He couldn't quite make out the rest of the sentence in the dark. It was smudged. And then it finished, "I decided to let the last one here live so he could tell people about my joke. After you tell 'em, tell 'em *Fuck you whoever you are!*' for me." And it was signed, "Silas Miner. The Old Man in the Hole."

Traveler tucked the note in his pocket, muttering, "What a *nasty* old man."

He moved out toward the entrance to the passage. He paused in the darkness, five feet from the entrance, blinking as he looked out into the fading flare of the day.

Rugg was looking at the entrance, then back at Link and Hill and Margolin, then back at the entrance to the passage.

Traveler checked the M16, switched off the safety. Crept closer to the entrance. Waited till Rugg was looking toward the entrance before shouting, "Get out of the way, Link!"

Link dove aside.

Rugg swung the AR180 toward the passage.

There was a rumbling sound from behind.

Traveler squeezed off a long burst from the M16, punching big red holes through Rugg's chest, knocking him backward. He fell twitching.

The AR180 fell near Margolin. Margolin reached out, and his fingers closed on the breach.

The rumbling came again. . . .

Traveler ran from the passage and into the sunlight, shouting, "Get away from the rocks!"

Hill helped Margolin to his feet. Link grabbed the

other M16 and the AR15. The four men moved down into the dead-end trail—and the heap of boulders fell in on itself, burying the passageway, covering the door to the vault with tons of rock.

They backed away. A few stones rattled out of the pile, but its outer edges held.

Then Link shouted, "The digmen!"

Four trapdoors were opening, men pouring out, carrying the Glory Boys' assault rifles.

Traveler and Link opened up on them, at the same time backing away to the cover of a large boulder to the side of the trail. Four of the digmen fell, but the others came on, firing. Bullets kicked up dust at Traveler's feet.

He and Link, Margolin and Hill ducked behind the boulder.

And then Margolin wrenched loose from Hill. "I don't wanna die lying in the dirt!" he shouted.

Margolin ran out into the open, firing the AR180 at the four digmen coming at him, spraying rounds with deadly accuracy, his years of experience giving him the edge.

All four men spun, shot to pieces, fell. But he kept going toward the trapdoors where more digmen warriors were emerging.

Traveler and Hill ran after him, shouting at him to stop, trying to cover for him.

But Margolin ran at the nearest trapdoor and, howling with insane glee. leaped into it feet first, knocking a man back down the ladder and disappearing inside, himself.

There was the sound of shooting and more gleeful howling and more shooting and gunsmoke rose from the trapdoors and Hill sobbed and ran to help and the heads of the digmen disappeared from the trapdoors as Margolin shot them from beneath and Traveler and Hill ran up to the underground entrances and—

It was quiet down there.

Margolin had killed or wounded most of them. Traveler and Hill mopped up the rest. Then they carried Margolin's limp, bullet-riddled body up the ladder and out to the sunlight.

They paused to look at the heap of boulders. Traveler passed the Old Man's note to the others. "You guys want to dig out all those boulders?"

One by one, they shook their heads. "Fuck it," Link said.

Margolin's death had soured the thing. And they knew that the Old Man must have some other nasty surprises waiting, down beneath. . . .

"I wonder what it was got smudged out on that note," Link murmured, as they carried Margolin's body down the trail.

After the rumbling stopped, and the vibrations ceased, the Spike stopped screaming for help. She tried the door again. Useless. She expended the shotgun load trying to blow it open. Hopeless. She raised the candle to read, once more, the words the old man had etched in gold on the wall.

"Here's the gold you wanted. You can have it forever. But forever won't be very long, maybe a month or so, even with the air holes, and the food I left for you, because the gold is radioactive. That's the way I found it and that's why I'm dying. There's a Geiger counter you can check it with. But I'm as good as my word—you can have the gold. Signed, *Silas Miner*. PS: I left the food so you could take longer dying. I hope you suffer bad.

And she did.

They put Margolin's body in the dragster. At Hill's insistence.

And Hill set it afire and rolled it off a cliff. "Viking funeral for a road fighter," he said.

"It was all for nothing," Traveler muttered later, as they drove the Meat Wagon down the road, heading for the highway south.

Rosalita sat quietly holding Link's hand. Looking at him worshipfully.

Link cleared his throat. "There *is* this . . ."

He pulled a bundle of rags from under the seat. He opened it. Inside were six plates of gold. "Took some off the roadrats, some off the army, some off the highwayman . . . my own . . . adds up to a considerable lump of gold . . . ."

Rosalita clapped her hands.

Traveler smiled. Then he scowled. "There's a Geiger counter in the glove compartment. Check that gold with it."

Link pulled the Geiger counter out and checked the gold, looking quizzically at Traveler the whole time. "What do you know that I don't know, pard?" Suddenly, he pulled the note that Traveler had taken from the skeletal hand out of his pocket and held it up to the light. "Whoa, when you hold this thing up to the light you can make out that last word—*radioactive.* 'The chamber is radioactive.' Jesus, Trav, the gold's hot. Could the old man have been lying?"

"I doubt it," Hill said. "He always had gold, from prospecting. This is probably from his prospecting gold. Lot of people carry Geiger counters. He wouldn't want anyone to set off one of those Geiger counters and warn them away from his little trap. No, you can bet the Spike is frying back there. . . ."

"Well . . ." Link looked at Traveler and Hill. Hill sat in the back. "There's a good lump of gold here. We'll share it equal. We could buy that boat. . . ."

Hill shook his head sadly. "I couldn't go without Bill. I don't want the gold, man."

Traveler said, "I've got business in the south, with a certain tribe of Indians." Jan's tribe. "You earned it, Link. Take it; find your way south. You and Rosalita. But if you do find civilization—get word back to us somehow."

Link nodded solemnly. "You got it, man."

Hill looked at Traveler. "Indians?"

"Indians," Traveler confirmed. "You going with me, Frank?"

Hill nodded. "And Bill's going with us too. I can feel him here, watching out for us."

Link looked at Traveler and shrugged. It's okay, the shrug said. He's got a right to be crazy.

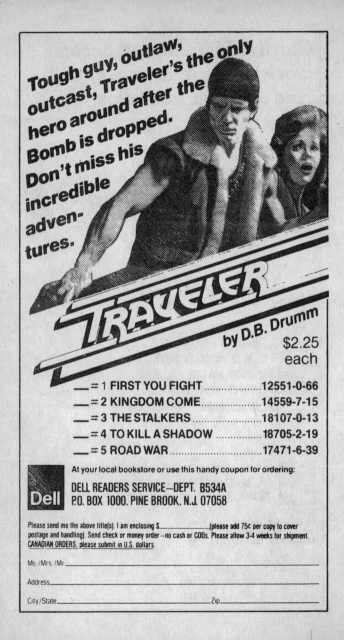

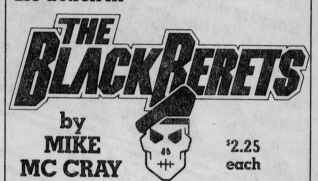